Because of Keith, Kit finally understands God's love. . .

Kit felt the warmth of his hand on her arm. He touched her without revulsion but with tenderness, and she knew suddenly that Keith's touch only reflected the tenderness that God felt for her too. Her tears spilled over. She felt as though a hard knot inside her, a knot that had been a part of her for years, was finally loosening, falling away, leaving her free. Her face lifted, she closed her eyes, feeling God's love wash over her.

Keith's hand slid down her arm and grasped hers. "Don't ever let people's rejection turn you against God, Kit. Remember, they even rejected Christ when He was here on earth. But people's opinions don't matter, not to God. He loves you. He cares for you." Keith hesitated, and when he spoke again, his voice was clipped. "I care too, Kit."

Kit blinked away her tears. "What?"

Keith's mouth twisted. "You heard me...."

CAROLYN R. SCHEIDIES makes her **Heartsong Presents** debut with the contemporary mystery, *To Be Strong*. Her work has appeared in many publications, and she is active in her church's puppet ministry, as well as the pro-life movement. Carolyn faces many of the same physical challenges as her heroine, with the same strong faith that her writing so clearly reveals.

To Be Strong

Carolyn R. Scheidies

Heartsong Presents

A note from the author:

This book is dedicated to my very real orthopedic surgeon and friend, Dr. Ken Ellis, and to all those who work at the Kearney Orthopedic and Fracture Clinic for their loving, Christian concern for each patient.

Other than Dr. Ellis, all characters in this book are fictional. The background of this story is drawn from my own rich Swedish heritage, but the tangled family relationships come only from my imagination.

I love to hear from my readers! Write to me at the following address:

Carolyn R. Scheidies
Author Relations
P.O. Box 719
Uhrichsville, OH 44683

Unless otherwise noted, all Scripture quotations are taken from the King James Version (KJV) of the Bible.

ISBN 1-55748-581-X

TO BE STRONG

PRINTED IN THE U.S.A.

one

*Finally, my brethren, be strong in the Lord,
and in the power of His might.* Ephesians 6:10

ଈ

Dr. Ken Ellis leaned back from the large desk that took up
most of his small but plush office in his new orthopedic
clinic. He tapped his long fingers against the desk's
wooden top, and behind his tan glasses, his eyes narrowed
with concern.

The wide blue eyes of the young woman opposite him
held his steadily. Her small, pointed chin was lifted, an
indication that she had already made up her mind. The
doctor knew that nothing short of physical force would
keep her from doing as she wished. He noticed how tight
her crooked fingers gripped the blue velvet of her chair
and the way her small body leaned toward him, as though
willing him to be convinced.

He smiled, but shook his head. "I don't like it, Kit.
You've just gotten off your crutches. This is no time to go
gallivanting off to Minneapolis by yourself. Minneapolis
is not Kearney, Nebraska, you know." He paused and
looked at her levelly. "How do you plan on accomplish-
ing this task, Kit?" He did not need to remind her of the
four years she had spent in reconstructive surgery. The
surgery had repaired damage left by the rheumatoid
arthritis she had had since she was thirteen. She might
still have it today, in fact, if her father had not taken her to
Texas.

In Texas a little known evangelist had prayed over her—and God had miraculously relieved her pain. Her fingers, however, remained just as gnarled, though the pain was gone, and her legs were as bent as ever. For months Kit had struggled with her faith after this partial healing. Eventually, she had decided that God was not done with her because she had failed Him in some fundamental way. Maybe she had not had enough faith, maybe she had been too selfish; she didn't know.

She looked away from Dr. Ellis' eyes and glanced down at her gnarled fingers. Her hands were a constant reminder of her failure as a person, as a Christian. But even more, though she hid this thought at the back of her mind, they reminded her of God's failure. If He truly loved her, why would He have given her this half-healing? And not only had He failed to completely heal her, He also had taken away both her mother and her father in the last two years, one through a stroke and one through a heart attack. This double blow had sent her spinning into a depression from which she was only now emerging.

For four years now she had struggled toward independence. Four years of surgery had given her a new set of knees, a new set of hips, and innumerable other small joints, but still her doctor hesitated over her ability to care for herself. His concern angered her. She would have liked to lash out at this doctor who had become her friend.

He was truly her friend, though, more than her doctor, and he had gone out of his way to see to her welfare, especially after her father's death. Dr. Ellis was the one who had found her an apartment with one of the nurses who worked in his office. Ruth had been Kit's friend since college days, and now she unobtrusively looked after Kit. Kit was grateful to Ruth; she was grateful to Dr. Ellis.

But still. . .

Her dependence haunted her. More than anything, she wanted to take care of herself, fend for herself. And now she had the chance. Gramma Clara wanted her to come to Minneapolis, and Aunt Augusta had begged her to come.

"She's dying, Katalina," Augusta had choked the other day on the phone. "She's dying. You must not disappoint her. You're all she has left now of Sophia. Your mother is gone, so you must go in her place. You must." Kit heard her aunt hesitate, a hesitation that was characteristic of every aspect of the tall, gaunt woman's life, and her voice lost its force and took on the tentativeness that was more common to her. "Pl. . .please come, Katalina. You will come? I did enclose a check which should more than cover your plane fare."

"Aunt Augusta," Kit had answered, "I want to come, you know I do, but I—I— Yes, I will come."

Now she felt herself grow more tense as she held herself perfectly still, determined not to fidget beneath Dr. Ellis' stare. "I have to go," she said. "There's no one else."

The doctor stood and paced the small space behind his desk. He glanced up at the shelves built into the wall, and for a moment he gazed at the picture of his wife Carolyn and their three children. Under the same circumstances, what would he say to his own daughter? He sighed and turned back to Kit.

"I don't like it. How are you going to climb into the plane? What about changing planes? How are you going to manage all that without assistance?" His eyes narrowed. "Is there someone who could go with you? If they're there to assist you, they don't have to pay full fare, you know."

Kit shook her head and her shoulders slumped. "There's no one. I tried. I know the problems." Her voice was defensive. "But I am going. One way or another, I'm going."

Ellis hid a smile. This determination of Kit's had served her well as she fought to learn again how to walk after being confined to a wheelchair for ten years, but her stubbornness was both her best friend and her worst enemy. Ellis swung around and punched a button on the multi-line phone on his desk. "Send in Dr. Long," he barked into the receiver.

Kit let go of the arms of her chair and clenched her fingers. "What are you doing?" Why was Ellis calling in Dr. Long? She could understand if he had asked for one of the other orthopedic doctors, but Dr. Long was a psychiatrist, the newest staff member at the Kearney Orthopedic and Fracture Clinic. He was another step in Dr. Ellis' dream to staff the clinic with doctors who were all professing Christians. But what did Dr. Long have to do with her?

She didn't have long to be in doubt. Five minutes later the door opened to admit the tallest man—outside of a few basketball players—Kit had ever seen. Dr. Long's head brushed the door frame as he entered, and his wide shoulders filled the doorway. A thatch of dark brown hair spilled into his gray eyes, and absently he shoved it out of his way. "You wanted to see me, Ken?"

Kit saw his eyes flick over her without interest before he turned back to Dr. Ellis. His respect for the older doctor was obvious in his face. Kit hid a smile as she watched the small, compact Dr. Ellis hurry to sit behind his desk, as though the large piece of furniture would lend him the same sense of presence that the taller man had.

"Dr. Long," he said, "I want you to meet a patient of mine. Katalina Anderson. Kit."

"Miss Anderson." Dr. Long gave a nod in Kit's direction. His eyes were cold and distant, yet she felt as though they pierced through her defenses and saw her more clearly than she wanted to be seen.

She squirmed in her chair and looked away from his gaze, thinking, "He must have learned to do that with his eyes because he's a shrink." She managed a smile and said, "How do you do, doctor." She turned to Dr. Ellis, her eyes questioning, waiting for him to explain why he had introduced Dr. Long to her.

Ellis leaned back in his chair, his eyes moving between the two young people who waited for him to speak. "Dr. Long," he said at last. "I know you have a conference in Minneapolis. When do you plan to leave?"

Kit stiffened. With a sinking feeling, she turned to the tall psychiatrist. "Monday morning," he said.

"I see." Dr. Ellis ran one finger along the edge of the desk. "I also understand you plan to stay with your sister and her family in the Minneapolis area—and you will be able to come and go as you please."

Dr. Long hesitated and then answered carefully, "Yes. When you hired me, I explained to you about this conference I had already planned."

"Of course." Ellis rubbed his hands. "Keith, I have a little problem. And I think you can help me solve it."

As Kit watched, Dr. Long's controlled expression gave no hint that he realized the other doctor's use of his first name put this conversation on a personal rather than professional level. He said merely, "I'm listening."

Ellis cleared his throat. "You may have heard me speak before of Miss Anderson here."

Kit looked down at her hands, but she could feel Dr. Long's gaze on her. The impersonal examination angered her, though he said nothing. She felt her face grow hot as she waited for his response.

"I have," he said at last.

Keith Long watched with interest as the color drained from the woman's cheeks, leaving her face paler than it was before. Few women blushed these days, he had observed. *A blush implied a certain innocence that most young women have lost,* he thought cynically, *before they left grade school.*

He watched her long dark lashes brush her pale cheeks as she continued to avoid his gaze. He did remember Ken Ellis discussing her case, and he realized she was more than just another patient to Ken, but he still did not understand where his colleague was heading.

Ellis was silent for a moment. In the short time since Dr. Long had joined their staff, Ellis had become familiar with the younger doctor's slow and silent evaluations, and he knew Keith always reached sensible conclusions. In fact, the man's insight was sometimes uncanny.

Dr. Ellis smiled and finally spoke. "Kit has a problem. Her grandmother—who may be dying—has asked her to come to Minneapolis to visit her. However," he clasped his hands and leaned forward in his chair, "Kit is unable to travel alone. I—"

"I haven't tried yet," Kit interrupted. Her face burned hotter than before. "If you would just—"

Dr. Ellis' voice overrode hers as though she had not spoken. "I have no intention of giving her my physician's permission for her to go unless she has someone along with her, someone willing to look out for her on the way there and back."

"I'm not a child," Kit said.

Dr. Long glanced at her. His face gave away no hint of

emotion, but she still thought she read the message that in his estimation she was just that: a child. Of course. He wasn't the only one to think that.

Keith watched the anger and frustration in the young woman's expression. He noticed her smooth oval face, her clear eyes, her sensitive lips, and he found he couldn't think of her as anything but an innocent, vulnerable child. Despite her anger, she reminded him of nothing more threatening than a fluffed-up kitten ready to spit. He held back a smile, reminding himself that she was showing little respect for the doctor who had graciously befriended her. "You want me to chaperon the young lady," he said, his voice level.

"Exactly. I'm sure you two will get along well." Ellis' eyes gleamed. "I have every confidence that you'll be able to keep Miss Anderson well in hand. In fact, I suspect she'll behave better for you than she does for me."

Kit's face flushed yet again as she listened to her doctor's chuckle, and she bit back an angry retort. The constant argument between herself and Dr. Ellis had always been friendly, a game, but would Dr. Long understand that? She found herself wanting the tall psychiatrist to think well of her, but as she looked at his face, the distant coolness she saw there seemed to tell her she had failed to impress him. She bit her lip and turned away.

For a moment she glared down at her hands as though they were the ones who had offended her. Well, maybe they had at that. If she were not crippled, she wouldn't have to submit herself to this humiliation. Obviously, Dr. Long wanted no part of Dr. Ellis' scheme. The man didn't look like he was the sort who would want to put himself out for someone like her.

She glanced again at his face, noting the clean, firm

lines of his brow and nose and chin. *Probably never had a sick day in his life,* she thought. She imagined him dining with tall, sophisticated, blond women, hiding his contempt for those who were less than perfect. . . Kit shook her head, reminding herself the man was a Christian. Dr. Ellis obviously trusted him, and she was wrong to condemn him before she knew him.

Keith watched the color ebb and flow in the girl's cheeks; he saw her shake her head, and he wondered what she was thinking. One corner of his mouth curled, and he drawled, "I think I can solve your problem, Ken. I'll have my secretary make Miss Anderson's reservations." He turned to Kit. "Miss Anderson—or Kit, if I may—I don't suppose you drive?"

Amused, he watched the girl swell up with indignation, and again he was reminded of a small cat. "I do too!" she said.

"Good. Then I needn't pick you up on Monday. I'll see you at the airport, shortly before eleven."

"I'll be there, Dr. Long," she said through tight lips. "That is if you're sure you want a 'problem' like me along." She bit her lip, wishing she could take back her words.

Dr. Long's eyes narrowed. Once again, he looked her over carefully. "I'm certain I'll be able to manage whatever problem you present," he said at last. He got to his feet. "I'll see you Monday."

Kit watched his quick stride out the door. She heard Dr. Ellis chuckle, and her face burned with humiliation.

two

Fear thou not; for I am with thee: be not dismayed;
for I am thy God: I will strengthen thee;
yea I will help thee; yea I will uphold thee
with the right hand of my righteousness. Isaiah 41:10

❧

Keith Long leaned back in his seat, watching the young woman on his right as she looked out the window. Since boarding the plane, she had avoided looking at him; she obviously had little desire for a chaperon. She twisted a narrow gold bracelet on her thin wrist, then played with the end of her long dark braid.

After a moment, she pushed the braid behind her shoulder, brushing Keith's arm as she did. He felt her stiffen and immediately lean further away from him. "I'm not going to bite," he drawled.

She glanced up at him, and he noticed her large blue eyes were fringed with the longest natural lashes he had ever seen. Her pale skin flushed, and he sensed her embarrassment was turning quickly to anger. "I'm well aware of that," she said and turned back to the window.

Kit's gnarled fingers clutched her slender purse. After a moment, she forced herself to turn away from the window, but she stared straight ahead at the seat in front of her, unable to face again his strange penetrating gaze.

Let the little minx keep to herself, Keith thought. *Fine with me.* He glanced sideways at her slender figure in the seat beside him, his eyes lingering on her small oval face.

13

He shook his head. *Hard to believe she's more than six-teen,* he thought, *let alone the twenty-one years she claims.* Her dark hair gleamed, he noted, and her lips had a sweet curve. *Her innocence is somewhat attractive,* he told him-self, and dismissed her from his mind.

He pulled a book from his briefcase and flipped it open. Thankfully, Kit seemed disinclined to chatter or flirt. The favor he was doing Dr. Ellis would have been even more tiresome if Kit had decided to practice her feminine wiles on him. Keith grimaced; she wouldn't have gotten far with him if she had tried.

Long ago he had, quite logically, determined what quali-ties he required in a woman—and little Miss Anderson certainly did not qualify. His mouth twisted as he recog-nized his own egotism, for Kit had done nothing to indi-cate she had any desire to attract him. Well, he was thank-ful for that. As he had thought before, this trip could have been a much greater burden on him if Kit had wanted to flirt with him. He turned a page in his book, and once again, he dismissed the girl from his mind.

He'd formed a habit, however, of measuring every woman he met against his list of requirements, and now, despite himself, he found himself studying the girl beside him, ticking off her qualities against his mental list. Too short, first of all; when she had greeted him at the airport earlier, he had noticed that her head barely reached his heart. And too thin; she'd been light as a feather when he had helped her up the steps to the plane. Third, although he had never heard her speak with anything that approached vulgarity, still she was too plain-spoken; the wife of an up-and-coming psychiatrist would require a certain degree of tact and sophistication. And last of all— he frowned—she looked nothing like he thought a woman should. Not only was she not blond, but her slender figure lacked the full curves he admired. She was too young. And her wide eyes were so blue, he could see her every thought mirrored there. . .

"Why do you always stare at me as though I were some sort of freak?"

Keith jumped. "K—Kit," he stuttered, embarrassed to have been caught staring. He looked away for a moment and then said smoothly, "Perhaps I'm merely trying to figure you out, Miss Anderson."

She looked at him, her eyes level, and then suddenly she smiled. He watched as her face changed from that of a solemn elf-child to—what? He couldn't think of an adequate metaphor.

"I *can* speak, you know," she said, her voice teasing. "If you want to know something about me, you only have to ask." Her blue gaze rested on his face, and she shook her head. "Now, why are you staring at me even harder than before?"

Reluctantly, he returned her smile. "I'm surprised to see that you can smile." He closed his book and waited to see what she would say next. *Perhaps the minx is going to flirt with me after all,* he thought, and his mouth twisted.

"Mm." Kit continued to look at him thoughtfully. "Your smile isn't so nice, you know. Do you enjoy frightening people?"

He raised an eyebrow. "Do I frighten you?"

"Well." She swallowed, wondering whether she should continue to speak honestly. "You are awfully big. I find that a little threatening. And when you look at me, I feel as though you can read my thoughts. I guess I find that disconcerting. I suppose it's a trick you learned as part of your profession."

Kit noticed that his smile reached his eyes this time. "Maybe so," he said. "Are you always so forthright?"

Kit shrugged. "I try to be honest." She looked down, then glanced up at him again quickly. "I'm sorry Dr. Ellis cornered you into this bit of babysitting. I know it must be a bother for you."

"I could have refused had I wanted."

"Sure you could have," Kit grinned, "and then Dr. Ellis would have thought you were a jerk."

He shrugged, and his smile widened into a grin. "Maybe." He paused and his face grew thoughtful. "Do you always put yourself down the way you just did?"

"What do you mean?"

"You referred to yourself as a bother. You labeled our companionship on this trip as babysitting. Do you truly think of yourself in those terms—or are you merely assuming this attitude to gain attention?"

Anger stained Kit's cheeks with color. "I am not a child looking for attention. You were the one who made it quite clear in Dr. Ellis' office that you considered me a problem to be handled and nothing more."

"If you recall, the word 'problem' was your own."

"And you echoed it."

She watched as a smile played at the corners of his mouth. "You haven't answered my question yet," he reminded her. "Do you truly think of yourself as a bother to others?"

Tears stung Kit's eyes. "Of course. How could I be anything else?" She turned once again toward the window, stretching her eyelids wide to keep the tears from spilling down her cheeks.

Below her, the earth looked like a toy model. Tiny trains chugged on toothpick tracks, and matchbox cars sped along a narrow black ribbon. Farm fields made a checker-board of green and brown squares.

Kit had a sudden dizzy realization of all the empty space between her and the earth. Everything that was solid, everything that was secure seemed to have dropped away beneath her, leaving her alone here in the sky with this strange young doctor. Even now, her gaze firmly turned away from him, she could sense his eyes on her. His presence filled her with turbulent new emotions, anger and confusion and fear, all mixed together, and something else, something to which she could put no name. He intrigued her, she had to admit, and in some strange way, against her will, she almost trusted him.

"Kit," he said softly. "Kit, look at me."

She raised her chin, determined not to obey the command in his voice.

"Please," he said, the note of authority now absent from his tone. She turned and watched his lips curve, the smile growing slowly until it filled his eyes. She couldn't help but smile back, though her stomach suddenly twisted.

For some reason, her mind was abruptly filled by the memory of his arms' warmth as he had carried her aboard the plane, and she felt her face grow warm. She jerked her shoulders, as though she could shake the thought away. Why did the arrogant man constantly make her blush, as though she were truly the child he thought her? She had never felt so young and inexperienced. Her mouth twisted, as she realized she was blaming the man for her own deficiencies. She had never had so much as a single date with a man, after all, so of course she would feel inexperienced in a man's company. That was hardly the doctor's fault.

The poor man was only doing Dr. Ellis a favor. In

Dr. Long's eyes, she must be nothing more than a little crippled girl with twisted hands and limping legs. She looked down at her hands and noticed that she had slid them beneath her purse, as though to hide them. Mentally, she shook her head at herself. By now she should have accepted her handicap.

But she hadn't. She hated being different from everyone else. She hated not being able to take care of herself, having to depend on the kindness of others. So often she had seen the instinctive pulling back in the face of someone she was meeting for the first time, felt the light touch on her hand rather than a firm handshake, and she always knew she would never fit in with people who had normal, healthy bodies. No, she would never be a whole person, she would always be a failure.

But Dr. Long, she realized, even when she first met him, had never made her feel that way. She cast a quick sidelong glance at him and wondered why.

"Kit." She heard the amusement in his voice. "I would like to be your friend. Truly."

She turned and stared at him. He raised one eyebrow. "Well?"

"You. . .really. . .wish to be my friend?"

"Does that surprise you so much?"

Kit nodded.

"Anyone would be privileged to know you, Kit. Why wouldn't they?"

Kit's face hardened. "You don't know what it's like to be inside this body. People look at me as though I were some sort of circus freak, not a real person at all."

"That's what you accused me of, wasn't it? But you were wrong."

Kit smiled at him shyly. "I'd like to be your friend.

Does that mean I'm no longer your 'problem,' Dr. Long?"

He laughed. "If we are going to be friends, how about calling me by my first name—Keith."

❧

During the rest of the plane trip, Kit tried to comply. At first she stumbled over his name and retreated behind her defenses. By the time their plane landed in Omaha, however, they were talking as comfortably as old friends.

Keith looked down at Kit as he carried her off the plane, surprised by how much he had enjoyed her company. This time, he noticed, she was relaxed in his arms, instead of stiff and tense, and carrying her down the steps was easier. He caught her grimace as he set her down on the other side of the gate, and he wondered whether it was caused by physical pain or emotional.

"Let's go get something to eat." He gave her no time to answer, but strode down the long hallway, halting only when he heard her labored breathing falling slightly behind him. Instantly, he stopped, and after she had caught her breath, he slowed his steps to hers.

When they had reached a restaurant and had found a booth, Kit took a bottle of arthritis-strength aspirin from her purse and popped two tablets in her mouth.

"So," Keith said, "that look you threw me when I put you down was caused by physical pain. I'm sorry."

"No, it wasn't that." Kit looked down into the glass of water in her hand. "I was just thinking how embarrassing it must be for you."

"Embarrassing for me, but not for you?"

Kit shrugged. "I'm used to it."

Beside them, the waitress cleared her throat. "What'll it be?"

Without consulting Kit, Keith ordered a large dinner

for both of them. Kit's lips tightened at his high-handedness. Mentally, she counted the cash she had with her. The meal would take more than she would have liked, but she could do little about it now.

Keith waited until the waitress had left and then leaned across the table toward Kit. "You're my guest," he said quietly. "And as for the other. . .I wasn't embarrassed. I've always felt that one need not be embarrassed for those things which are unavoidable."

"I never thought of it like that," Kit said, her eyes still on her water glass. "I know I embarrass some people. They don't know what to do or say. Sometimes I can make things better by just talking to them, helping them to feel more comfortable. But other times. . ." She blinked, disturbed that on such short acquaintance she should feel the longing to confide in this man. Even with Dr. Ellis, whom she liked and trusted, she seldom shared anything deeper than her physical problems. Maybe Keith had a knack for pulling inner feelings to the surface because of his profession. Still, she felt uncomfortable. She put her hands beneath the table and wished she could hide her face from his gaze as well.

He reached across and pulled her hand back onto the table. "Don't let your physical condition dictate who you are, Kit. You are a child of God, a child of the King of kings, the Lord of lords. All His children are worthy of respect and love. Even if others are too blind to realize that, you must respect yourself. If you do, you'll find others will too. What's important is who you are inside. And, Kit Anderson," his gray eyes smiled into hers, "I have a feeling that the person you're hiding away, afraid of being hurt, is a person worth knowing."

Kit gaped at him, surprised by the warmth in his voice.

She felt as though he'd stripped her bare, then wrapped her lovingly in warm clothes.

She was relieved when the waitress arrived with their plates, giving her an excuse not to answer. She looked at the steak on her plate with misgiving, knowing how embarrassing sawing at a tough piece of meat could be, her hands too weak to slice it. When she picked up the steak knife, however, she found that the cut of meat was so tender that the knife slid through it. She put a bite in her mouth.

Keith smiled, watching her delight with the meal. *No wonder,* he thought, *that Dr. Ellis thinks of her almost as his daughter.*

Soon, they returned to the plane for the last leg of their trip to Minneapolis. After the large meal, Kit was sleepy. Again and again, her head drifted downward until it hit the window ledge, making her jerk awake.

At last, Keith smiled indulgently and wrapped a long arm around her shoulders. He pulled her head against his own shoulder. For a moment she stiffened, but soon she sighed and relaxed. He looked down at the long dark lashes that lay against the pale skin of her cheeks and watched her sleep. Dr. Ellis must feel the same way about her, he told himself; her innocence and vulnerability would bring out the father in any caring man.

Surely, he told himself, *that explained the pleasure he felt now, holding her warmth against him.*

three

*I can do all things through Christ
which strengtheneth me.* Philippians 4:13

❧

Kit woke slowly, feeling more warm and secure than she
had in a long time. Drowsily, she realized she was still
held tight in the circle of Dr. Long's arm, but she could
not bring herself to pull away. Instead, she let her head
rest on his shoulder while her mind wandered ahead to
Minneapolis, to the small house where her Aunt Augusta
and Gramma Clara waited for her.

If Kit's mother Sophia were still alive, she would be
the one flying to her stepmother's side now. Her mother,
Kit knew, would have been as calm and capable as she
always was, able to handle any crisis. By comparison,
Kit felt inadequate, but her mother was gone now. Her
grandmother and aunt would have to make do with Kit.

Aunt Augusta had sounded so strange on the phone, so
nervous. . .but then, Aunt Augusta had always been, well,
a bit peculiar. She had begged Kit to honor her Gramma
Clara's dying request, a request that made little sense to
Kit. As Aunt Augusta had asked, Kit had brought the flat
mahogany jewelry case, the one that had belonged to her
mother and her mother before her, but Kit failed to see
what good it could possibly do. Why would Gramma Clara
want to see the jewelry box?

Behind her closed lids, Kit pictured the night her mother
had collapsed and died of a massive cerebral hemorrhage.

Kit had stroked the cool surface of the box over and over, as though it were a living thing. Her mother had always cherished the box with its worn, red velvet interior, and just touching the box always gave Kit a sense of loving roots anchoring her to the past.

"This jewelry box," her mother once told her, "has been in my family for generations." Now it belonged to Kit as it had belonged to her mother, and her mother before that.

Gramma Clara was not Sophia's real mother but her stepmother, so why would she be interested in the box? Kit shook her head slightly, and Dr. Long's blazer brushed against her cheek, distracting her from thoughts of her family.

The plane shuddered, and Kit knew it must be settling into its landing pattern over Minneapolis. She forced herself to pull away from the doctor's warmth and sit up. She yawned, then blushed as she met Dr. Long's eyes.

"Feel better now?" He removed his arm from her shoulders.

"Much. . .Ah, thanks." Kit looked away from his eyes.

He chuckled. "My pleasure, miss."

Wishing she could control the warmth that rushed to her face, Kit turned to stare out the window. She watched the city rushing up toward her, the buildings growing bigger and bigger, the cars less and less like toys. The plane's massive engines thundered, and she yawned wide, trying to relieve the pressure in her ears.

She hadn't seen Minneapolis for seven years. Like yesterday, though, she remembered her father driving her here. She hadn't wanted to come. She hadn't wanted to go for treatment to Sister Kenny's Institute, a rehabilitation center.

She remembered how small she had felt back then in

the undersized wheelchair she was too weak to push for herself. The time she had been at the institute had been good for her, though; she had made new friends and learned to dress herself, even comb her own hair and pull on her socks. But she hadn't learned to walk again, and her mother and father had been as disappointed as she was.

Only Dr. Ellis had been able to help her walk. Kit tried to stretch her legs out in front of her, wondering if she'd be able to stand after being cramped for so long. She rubbed her knee beneath her pantleg, feeling the long scar. A matching scar marked her other knee and both her hips, and they itched now. But though her legs weren't perfect, being able to walk again was well worth the painful surgery and therapy.

Happiness bubbled up inside her. Watching her, Keith saw the joy that flashed across her face, then just as quickly disappeared. "What's wrong?"

She twisted the gold band on her wrist. "I was suddenly so glad just to be alive. . .but Gramma Clara. . . Poor Gramma Clara. Poor Aunt Augusta." She sighed, and then a look of panic crossed her face. "I wonder who will pick me up?"

"Doesn't your aunt drive?"

Kit shook her head. "She never did. I hope they remember to send someone."

Keith squeezed her hand, and Kit was surprised by his firm touch on her fingers, a touch that held no hint of revulsion. "Don't worry," he said. "I'll see you get to your grandmother's house. I won't let the wolf get you, Little Red Riding Hood." His gray eyes smiled into hers. Kit let out her breath and smiled back.

The plane landed and taxied to a stop. Keith reached over and unbuckled Kit's seat belt. His lips twisted as he realized what he had done; sensitivity wasn't one of the qualities he credited to himself, and he felt a sort of uneasy surprise now as he recognized that he had anticipated Kit's need before she had even asked.

Keith stood up and turned to help Kit, but the stewardess moved quickly to his side. "Please wait. It will be easier to wait until the others have deplaned."

Kit sank back gratefully, glad to have her departure witnessed by as few persons as possible, but a frown of annoyance crossed the doctor's face at the delay. The other passengers hurried past them, while Dr. Long shifted impatiently.

Finally, the stewardess returned. "You may leave now. May I help you, miss?"

Keith unfolded his long legs, stood, and bumped his head on the ceiling. Kit hid a smile as he ducked down. "Thank you," he said, "but I can take care of her." A smile barely touched the corners of his mouth.

"Anything I can do to help?"

Keith glanced at the stewardess, noticing her blond hair and full figure with approval. "Yes. You can hang onto this for me." He handed her his briefcase.

He turned back to Kit and took the small hand she held up to him. When he pulled her to her feet, she swayed for a moment, and his large hands spanned her waist to steady her. The heat rose in her face. "Sorry," she muttered. "It takes me a while to get balanced and moving again."

Keith grinned and his hands settled more firmly around her waist. "I don't mind. Happy to be of service, milady."

Kit saw the gleam of gentle amusement in his eyes, and she wondered how she had ever thought him humorless. His warm hands steadied her as she gingerly took a step forward. Her joints limbered, and she grew confident enough to move away a little, her face still burning.

At the plane's narrow doorway, however, she hesitated, looking down at the steep steps. She would have liked to manage them on her own, but when she glanced up at the doctor, he grinned and raised one eyebrow, then picked her up in his arms. He descended the stairs and did not set her down again until they were inside the building.

As he put her down, the stewardess held out his briefcase. "Your case," she said and smiled into his face, her lips parting to show white straight teeth. Her eyes flicked over him. "I'm laying over for a couple of days in Minneapolis." She raised her well-shaped brows and waited for his answer.

Kit looked at the doctor, waiting for his answer. "I hope you'll enjoy your rest," he said at last, his voice courteously level.

The woman's eyes flashed. "I'm sure I will." She took her leave politely enough, but Kit noticed the angry flounce of her hips as she marched away.

"She's a bit put out," Kit commented.

"No reason she should be."

"You didn't notice she was—um, interested?"

Keith glanced down at Kit, and one corner of his mouth quirked upward. "I noticed. However, she was not, ah, not my type."

Kit sniffed. "I would have thought she was every man's type."

Keith's grin widened. "There are other considerations in assessing a woman than appearance." He tried to put a stern note in his voice, wanting to underline for his own benefit Kit's lack of experience, but the fact was, her observation had startled him. Just a few hours ago, as he had run over his requirements in a woman, a figure like

the stewardess' had seemed essential to him—and yet he
had spoken the truth now when he said she was not his
type.

He cleared his throat. "I suppose we need to see if you
have a ride."

"Yes," Kit murmured. Suddenly, she couldn't meet the
doctor's eyes. All her brave talk about being able to come
to Minneapolis on her own, and here she was dependent
on Keith's help for every move. She would never have
been able to manage on her own. As always, her lack of
independence filled her with frustration and embarrassment, and yet the gratitude she felt toward Keith was warm
and comforting.

In their short time together, she had confided more to
him than she had to any of her other friends, friends she'd
known for years. Always before, something had held her
back, keeping her from reaching out beyond her defenses.
She smiled and shook her head. After all, Dr. Long did
this sort of thing for a living; no wonder she felt comfortable confiding in him.

"Katalina. Katalina Anderson."

Kit turned and looked up into the coldest blue eyes she
had ever seen. "I'm Katalina," she said. She looked at the
middle-aged man's blood-shot eyes, red nose, and the large
paunch that sagged on his small frame. "Who are you?"

"Lars. Lars Bergstrom." He nodded, his mouth twist-
ing in a smile that didn't reach his eyes. "Your dear aunt
sent me to pick you up."

"How do you do, Lars," Kit said politely, but inside she
groaned. Gramma Clara had told her about this cousin of
sorts, a n'er-do-well who had never held a steady job.

Mentally, Kit scolded herself for once again judging
someone harshly. She smiled. "Lars, this is Dr. Long

who. . ." She fell silent, uncertain how to explain the doctor's presence.

Dr. Long stuck out his big hand and shook Lars' limp one. "Since I had a conference in town, we thought it would be nice to keep each other company on the trip." He looked at Kit, and one eyelid drooped in a barely perceptible wink. She smiled at him gratefully.

"So you're here to pick Kit up?" the doctor asked Lars.

Lars nodded. "Where's your stuff? I wanta get going."

Keith frowned, then turned to Kit. "If I may, let me take your suitcase to the car." He was rewarded with another smile.

Lars strode ahead of them, ignoring both his cousin and the doctor. Keith carefully paced his strides to Kit's, and Lars soon outdistanced them. Kit tried to keep up, but her sides ached with the effort.

Around her, metal clanged against metal, people shouted, planes roared, hemming her in with noise. She had forgotten the city's constant discord, and now she would have liked to cover her ears to shut out the noise.

She grimaced, both from the din and from her shortness of breath. Keith took her arm to steady her as she stood at the baggage counter, panting for breath. Their luggage arrived safely, and before Kit had managed to get her breath back, Lars whipped away from the counter and strode down the long corridor to his car.

Keith picked up his two suitcases and tucked Kit's small one under his arm. He tried to juggle his briefcase as well until Kit reached out and took it from him. "I can take that," she said, her eyes gleaming with anger at her cousin's rudeness.

Outside, Lars already had the motor running in his dusty Skylark. He stared straight ahead, waiting for them, not bothering to even lean over to open a door.

Keith hesitated a moment before he set down his luggage. His eyes flashed as he looked at the back of Lars' head, but at last Keith put Kit's case in the back seat and opened the front door for her. He noticed the dust that clung to the door, the dashboard, even the rearview mirror, and he almost pulled Kit back. The man was her cousin, though, and he'd been sent to pick her up, so Keith helped Kit settle into the car's dusty interior.

She handed his briefcase up to him, then bit her lip, her eyes wide and worried.

"I'll call," he assured her. "Give me your aunt's name again."

Kit gave it to him, then watched as Keith shut the door. He went around the car and leaned down to look into Lars' open window. "Nice to meet you, Mr. Bergstrom."

Lars mumbled an answer, then revved the engine impatiently. Kit looked after Keith's tall back as he walked away, her face burning with humiliation at her cousin's behavior. Why had Aunt Augusta sent him, of all people?

Out of the corner of her eye, she surveyed him. He looked more than twice the age of Dr. Long, though she knew the age difference was actually not that great. From what she had heard, though, Lars' years of indulgent living had aged him prematurely.

He snorted. "You're wondering where I fit in, aren't you? I don't fit the pretty family picture, huh?" He had pulled onto the highway, but he looked at her, rather than the road, his mouth twisted in a sneer.

Kit shrugged. "No, you don't."

He appeared startled by her honesty. "You don't remember me then?"

She shook her head.

"Well, I'm Edmund's son."

"I remember. Edmund is Gramma Clara's brother. But I don't remember ever meeting you before."

"Not likely you would have." Lars gave a bark of laughter. "The family don't have much to do with me if they can help it."

Kit changed the subject. "How is Gramma?"

"Old lady's holding her own. Too stubborn to kick off, I guess. But when she does," Lars licked his lips, "all that silver and the rest of her estate goes to her next of kin. The rest of them may not like it, but that includes yours truly. So I'm holding my breath waiting for the old girl to go."

Kit turned to study Lars' hard features. The threatening thrust of his body behind the steering wheel sent a chill down her spine.

She gulped back her fear. "And your father, how is he?"

"Weak as ever. With Clara on the edge, all the old man does is sit in the corner of her living room, turning this dumb hourglass over and over. Drives me bats."

"He loves his sister."

Lars grunted, then turned to look at her again. "Well, so why'd you come?"

"I came to see Gramma."

"Sure. What're you hoping to get out of her?"

"Nothing!" Kit pressed her lips together. "I think your attitude is uncalled for."

Lars laughed. "Spunky, huh? Didn't think someone like you. . .the way you are. . .would have it in you. But I've gotta tell you, you don't have much chance with the old lady. She hardly knows you."

Kit's stomach twisted with anger. "Maybe not, but I care about her. She is my grandmother after all. And she asked to see me."

"Stepgrandmother," Lars corrected. "And the old lady is too far out of it to have asked anyone to come. You're making that up."

Kit sighed. "She had Aunt Augusta call me. I think she really wanted my mother, though." She swallowed the tears that stung her eyes, determined not to cry in front of this man.

"Why would she want to see you?"

Kit shrugged. "I don't know yet."

"If that old woman thinks she's going to cut her real family out of her will. . ." Kit heard the threat in his voice.

"Are you so certain you're already in Gramma Clara's will?" she asked him, keeping her voice cool and level.

"Who knows for sure. But I can tell you one thing. No cripple's going to do me out of what's mine."

Kit bit back her disgust. After a moment she said, "I have no idea what Gramma Clara has in her will, or if she even has one. Frankly, I don't care. I don't know why she asked for me, except that I too am family. And if what I think should count for anything, then it's my belief that Aunt Augusta should get 'most everything when Gramma dies. After all, Aunt Augusta is the one who's stayed with Gramma all these years."

Lars snorted. "You mean Clara has been taking care of her all these years."

Kit turned away from him, afraid if she said any more she would not be able to control her anger.

*

Meanwhile, Keith Long compared the clean interior of his taxi with Kit's transportation. He had a nagging feeling that he should have taken Kit with him and sent Lars on his way. He couldn't shake the anxious look in Kit's wide eyes out of his mind. He hated imagining her alone with that cousin of hers.

He shook his head sharply. Kit Anderson was no longer his concern. He had a conference to attend.

four

*She also lieth in wait as for a prey, and increaseth
the transgressors among men.* **Proverbs 23:28**

❧

As Lars pulled onto the tree-lined avenue, Kit sighed,
relieved to be off the freeway. She leaned forward to see
the quiet neighborhood's modest houses, hoping to see
something familiar, something that would tell her the uncomfortable ride was almost over.

At last she saw the small, white, two-story house, as
tidy as an English cottage, its bushes trimmed and the
lawn recently cut. The house, Kit knew, reflected Aunt
Augusta's craving for perfection.

Lars pulled into the driveway. He waved at the well-
kept lawn. "Now that Dad isn't well enough to help
Augusta with the house and lawn, she actually expects
me to help her." He shook his head. "Digging up weeds
isn't quite my idea of a good time."

Kit glanced at his soft, white hands on the steering wheel.
"No, I imagine it wouldn't be. But I don't see why you
can't help out."

"Why should I? Why should she think she's entitled to
free help? Let her hire someone like everybody else. It's
not like she's ready for the poorhouse."

Kit shook her head and turned her face away from her
cousin.

Lars turned off the car's engine. He opened his door
and, without a backward glance, made his way across the

lawn to the house. Kit opened her mouth, then shut it again. She didn't really want the man's help anyway.

She stared at the door, waiting for her aunt to come fluttering out. Although she hadn't been here for several years, Kit could visualize the bungalow's interior, the unfinished second floor that was just one long storage room under the eaves, the cozy living room and tiny kitchen downstairs, the two bedrooms, and shining bath. Could she manage to get inside without help?

Tentatively, she curled her fingers around the door handle. Once she had gotten her fingers caught in the handle of a car door, much to her embarrassment, but usually she didn't even have enough strength in her wrist to pull the handle. The inside of the car was growing hot and muggy, though, so she pulled the handle as hard as she could. "Help me, Lord. Please help me open the door."

Her fingers aching, Kit gave one last hard jerk that wrenched her wrist. The door swung open. "Thanks," she breathed. She kicked the door wide, swung out her legs, and put her weight on her feet. Keeping one hand on the car, she heaved herself up onto the curb. She turned to shut the door, almost losing her balance as she did, but she steadied herself and walked forward, smiling at her accomplishment.

She limped up the sidewalk, eyeing the steps ahead. Gingerly, she put her hand on the wrought iron railing. Solid. Kit took a breath and surprised herself by easily negotiating the shallow steps to the front door.

Ignoring the doorbell, Kit opened the door and walked into the house. After the bright sunlight, she blinked in the sudden darkness. After a moment, as her eyes adjusted to the gloom, she could see that the blinds were down, the curtains drawn.

Lars lounged before her on a sofa. "See you finally made it inside."

Kit looked at him. "No thanks to you. Why didn't you stay and help me?"

"You made it on your own, didn't you?"

"And if I hadn't been able to?"

He shrugged, his eyes sliding up and down her body. Even in the shadows, Kit could read the revulsion in his face. "Don't expect pampering around here. Ain't no hospital."

Kit rubbed the wrist she'd pulled when she opened the car door, and she gritted her teeth to hold back an angry reply. She opened her mouth, unable to contain her anger any longer, when a small movement in the corner of the room caught her eye.

She took a step forward and squinted at the pale, shrunken little man in the corner. He moved his head, and a sliver of light from between the blinds caught his eyes with an odd gleam.

"Uncle Edmund?"

The tiny man's head bobbed, his eyes glinting.

"Uncle Edmund, why is it so dark in here? It's the middle of the afternoon. Let me open the curtains."

"No!" The strength of the cracked voice startled her.

"My dear father doesn't much care for light. Do ya, Dad?" There was an undertone to Lars' voice that Kit didn't understand.

Kit shook her head, trying to dispel the feeling that she had wandered into a circus fun house—or a nightmare. "You're sure?"

Neither of the two men answered her, and after a moment she cleared her throat. "Where's Aunt Augusta?"

At that moment, a large, round-faced woman strode

heavily into the room. "Your aunt is still at work," she said cheerily. "She'll be home around five, five-thirty, depending on the traffic. She takes the bus, you know." She smiled and stuck out a large, calloused hand. "I'm Sally Callen, Clara's private nurse. And you're Katalina."

"Kit." She felt her hand enveloped in the woman's warm, firm grip, and she smiled gratefully. "Nice to meet you, Ms. Callen. How is Gramma? May I see her?"

"Sally, dearie, everyone calls me Sally. And I'm afraid you'll have to wait to see your grandmother. She's sleeping right now." The nurse narrowed her eyes at the other two in the room, and then took a step closer to Kit. "You just come on into the kitchen with me," she said, her voice lowered. "I have some hot water all ready for tea. You can join me."

"Thank you, Sally. I'd like that." She followed the nurse through the dining room to the kitchen, thankful to leave the living room's gloom behind.

She managed to climb onto a stool beside the small kitchen table, and then, glancing around the homey little room, she relaxed. Sunlight poured through the window across the blue and yellow Swedish decor, while Sally bustled about, reminding Kit of her mother.

"Would you prefer coffee?" Sally asked. "I know most Swedes do."

Kit shook her head. "Tea's fine. I'm afraid I never developed a taste for coffee. Actually, I prefer herb teas when I can get them." She watched as Sally set two blue Wedgewood cups on the table with a tea bag in each. "What about you? You don't like coffee either?"

Sally laughed. "Never touch the stuff. Must be because there's not a drop of Swedish blood in my veins. Not like most of the people around here." She turned to the stove.

"Water's ready. Do you want sugar?" She poured the bubbling water into the cups.

"No, thanks." Kit snuggled her hands around the cup and watched as Sally settled her large frame in one of the small kitchen chairs. Kit raised the cup to her lips, then set it down. "I'm afraid it'll be some time before this cools down to my tolerance level." She looked thoughtfully at Sally's cheerful, round face. "Does Uncle Edmund ever do anything besides sit in that chair? Lars told me that's all he does."

Sally snorted. "As though Lars does much more himself. Those two. Real pair, aren't they?"

"Lars wasn't particularly friendly to me."

"He never is. I don't think even Edmund cares much for him, for all he's his own son."

Kit's eyes darkened with compassion. "No wonder Lars is the way he is, if his own father doesn't care about him. He's so. . .so surly. Has he always been like that, do you know?"

Sally shrugged her heavy shoulders. "He's been pretty much the same for as long as I've known him—and I was around while he was growing up. Seems likes he's worse now, though. He'd been gone for several years, you know, but when he heard about Clara's condition he came back. Now he and his father do nothing but wait in that dark living room like a couple of vultures."

Kit shook her head. "Lars wants Gramma to die, doesn't he? He's already making plans for his part of the estate. He seems to think I came here just to steal his part of the inheritance." She sniffed. "The idea, that I would want to rip off Gramma!"

Sally's eyes narrowed. "Do you know how much your grandmother will leave?"

Kit shrugged. "She's not wealthy. But she has lots of fine old china, some silver tea sets, oak chests, antique furniture, all the hand-embroidered linen. I don't know. I think the house is in Aunt Augusta's name. Do you know?"

Sally nodded. "That's right." She took a sip of her tea. "Lars say anything else?"

"Not really. I'm sure Gramma will leave both him and Uncle Edmund something—but like I told Lars, Augusta has been the one taking care of Gramma all these years. She should get 'most everything."

Sally's eyes smiled at Kit over the rim of her cup. "Your visit is a surprise, you know. Why *did* you come?" She looked at Kit's face and then patted her hand. "Don't worry, I'm not going to accuse you of gold-digging."

Kit set down her teacup. "Gramma asked for me."

"Did she say why?"

"No, not really. But I think it's because I'm the closest she can get to my mother."

Sally reached across the table and again patted Kit's hand. "I'm sorry about your mother."

Tears stung Kit's eyes at the woman's unexpected sympathy, and Sally's fingers closed over hers. "I see you have your mother's sensitivity," she said.

Kit looked up. "You knew my mother well?"

"Yes, I did." Sally smiled. "I knew her before that dashing young minister swept her off her feet, married her, and carried her off from us. We lost contact over the years, but I'm delighted now to meet her daughter. You remind me of her, dearie. The same deep blue eyes, though yours are large like your father's. You have her ready smile too—though not her plump figure. You must have taken after your slim father."

"I suppose I did. Food did tend to settle on Mother's bones."

"Like it does on mine." Sally patted her ample bosom, and they both laughed.

"Oh, Sally," Kit whispered, "after that terrible car ride with Lars, it's such a relief to meet you."

"Well, I'm here most days. Clara needs constant attention now."

"Then you stay the night?"

"Oh, no. I have an apartment on Nicolette. Augusta keeps pretty close watch on her mother when she's home."

"How long have you been caring for Gramma?"

"Several months now. Like I said, I'd lost touch with Sophia, your mother, but Augusta and I have always been close. When her mother needed a nurse, Augusta turned to me, but before that I'd been helping out in this family in one way or another for years."

Kit drank the last of her tea. "It's hard for me to imagine you and Aunt Augusta as friends. You're so different."

Sally's chin shook as she chuckled. "I know. She's a perfectionist—and I'm just the opposite. She went to finishing school—and I had to do housekeeping jobs to pay for my nurse's training."

Kit smiled. "And Aunt Augusta ended up as an executive secretary and you a nurse. As far as I'm concerned, you've got the more impressive profession."

Sally shrugged. "Maybe. But over the years Augusta has earned perks that would never be available to a nurse, including a good chunk of prime stock. She works in that IDS Tower, you know, the tallest building in Minneapolis. Meanwhile, I move from job to job, without so much as a thank you half the time."

Kit thought she heard a note of jealousy in Sally's voice, but when she looked into her face, it was as pleasant and unlined as ever. Kit turned her teacup round and round between her fingers. "I have a hard time imagining Augusta as a decisive secretary," she said. "She's not at all like that whenever I've seen her. When she used to visit us, she'd drive Mom to distraction, never being able to make up her mind about anything. She wouldn't even be able to decide whether to take a bus or a plane home, unless someone stepped in and made the decision for her." Kit shook her head. "But she's certainly stuck by Gramma Clara all these years. That must have been a heavy burden, especially now that Gramma's been so sick."

Sally's lips tightened. "Dearie, she stuck by your gramma because she was just that—stuck. Stuck in a rut. She could never decide whether to marry or not—and she had some pretty good offers in her day, let me tell you. If I'd been in her shoes, I'd have snatched one of those men up in a second, but your aunt was too scared to take a chance."

Kit thought about her aunt, imagining her tall, angular figure, her well-cut but conservative clothes, the anxiety that always lurked in her eyes. "Poor Aunt Augusta," she said. "Mama told me once that Aunt Augusta was afraid any man she married would die and leave her stranded and alone. She didn't want to risk that pain. And when Mama died, Aunt Augusta went to pieces. She talked to me after the funeral—and she was terrified. Mom didn't live close to her, but Aunt Augusta seemed to have always clung to her emotionally. I suppose because Mama was the older sister."

"Half-sister," Sally corrected quickly.

Kit looked at her thoughtfully, trying to put a label to the tone she heard in Sally's voice. "Well," she said at last, "with Gramma Clara dying, I can imagine that Aunt

Augusta is going through a hard time now."

Sally swallowed the last of her tea. "Poor Augusta." She shook her head and poured herself another cup.

"I can understand some of her fear," Kit said. "I admit the thought of flying to Minneapolis alone was scary for me. But——" Her face softened as she thought of Keith and how easy he had made the trip for her.

"Left behind someone special?" Sally guessed.

Kit blushed and shook her head. "No. Nothing like that." She looked down at her twisted fingers and the smile faded from her lips. "I have lots of friends, but. . .no one special. Who'd want to be stuck with my problems for life?" She cleared her throat and quickly changed the subject. "What about you? Are you married?"

"Nope. Came close only once." Sally looked down at her bulk and grimaced. "Who'd want to be stuck with this figure?" She laughed ruefully.

Kit grinned. "I guess we make a good pair. I just can't imagine anyone loving me the way I am. Not that God hasn't been good to me. At least I can walk now."

Sally nodded. "Clara was so pleased about that. She's always talked a lot about your progress. Your mother's letters and now yours were very important to her." Sally set down her cup and frowned. "There's something different now, though, about her interest in you. She has something on her mind. She may be dying, but she's sharp as ever, so don't let them tell you that she's just confused." Sally snorted. "She's not like that Edmund." She hesitated, then looked across the table at Kit. "Maybe. . .maybe you'll be able to find out what it is that's bothering your gramma's mind. You know, dearie, it would be such a help to her if you could relieve her of whatever it is that's troubling her. So if you can find out anything. . ."

Kit nodded, but she already knew that whatever was bothering Gramma had something to do with the jewelry box. She thought of the box, tucked safely inside her suitcase—and then remembered that her suitcase was still in Lars' car.

"My suitcase—" she started to say but broke off as Augusta unlocked the back door and strode briskly into the kitchen. The further she came into the house, the more her steps slowed, until she hesitated, then stopped. Watching her, Kit thought she could see the guise of a successful career woman dropping from her shoulders, revealing the familiar indecisive and fearful old maid beneath.

"Kit, *goddag. Hur star det till*? You are well? You got here all right? And your luggage, did Lars put it in my bedroom as I told him?"

"Hello, Aunt Augusta. I'm fine and the trip was pleasant. But my suitcase is still in Lars' car."

Kit followed Aunt Augusta into the living room. "Lars, please bring Kit's bag into the house as soon as possible. I can't think why you didn't do it before."

Lars stared sullenly up at the tall woman. "I'll get to it."

Augusta turned to her uncle. "Please, Uncle Edmund. Tell Lars to get the bags. I know Kit would like to get settled in before dinner. It's not courteous to her to leave her bags out there in the car."

Edmund turned his glittering eyes on his son. "You heard her, Lars."

Lars looked back at his father for a moment, and tension crackled in the dark room. At last Lars grunted and rolled to his feet. "Okay, okay. Don't get your dander up. I'll get 'em."

His worn jeans sagged around his hips as he lumbered

out the door, but Kit noticed that the unlaced sneakers he wore were a designer brand.

"Well," said Aunt Augusta. "I'll help you get settled, Kit."

She led the way to her bedroom. Kit remembered the twin beds with their rose spreads, the rose wallpaper, the rose-crocheted doilies which decorated the lamp stand and chest of drawers. Even the scent of lilacs, at odds with the room's roses, was familiar.

Her aunt reached a long, tapered hand to smooth the spread on the bed closest to the door. "This one will be yours. It's a few steps closer to the bathroom. Can—can I help you put your things away?"

Carefully, Kit lowered herself onto the bed, then swung forward and up again. She breathed a sigh of relief. Some beds were too low for her to push herself out of once she was on them, but this one she could manage.

Without knocking, Lars shoved her small suitcase through the door. "Here. That better be all."

"Thank you, Lars," Augusta called after him. She turned to her niece. "Please let me help you unpack."

Kit hesitated. "Why don't I just hand you the things that need hanging up?" She clicked open the case. For some reason, she didn't want to talk to her aunt yet about the jewelry box.

She unfolded a long navy skirt and matching jacket, then a silky white blouse, and handed them to her aunt. Augusta looked them over. "This all you have?" her aunt asked. "We do dress for dinner, you know."

Silently, Kit pulled out a burgundy silk blouse which would also go with the navy suit, then a royal blue dress. Her aunt took them. "This is it?"

Kit looked at her aunt's expensive suit, something Kit

could never have afforded, and bit back her answer. After all, for all that her aunt's clothes were more costly than her own, and certainly more numerous also, her aunt's clothes always looked slightly dated. Their colors were drab, her blouses plain and childish. Even her hair was drab, Kit thought, always styled in the short, tight curls of another generation. Her aunt's thin lips had never worn so much as a touch of lipstick, and her pale cheeks were never blushed with cosmetics. *Poor Aunt Augusta,* Kit thought, and her anger evaporated.

She smiled. "If you tell me where, I'll put the rest in a drawer."

Augusta glanced nervously at her niece's casual pants and shirt. Kit knew her aunt never wore pants herself, but Augusta said nothing, only pulled open a drawer. "You can use this. Is it all right? Is it low enough? Or no, maybe it's too heavy. I should have emptied another drawer. It won't take me a minute—"

"No," Kit interrupted, trying to keep her irritation from her voice. "Thanks. This one is just fine. I can handle the rest of the unpacking, Aunt Augusta. Thank you."

Quickly, she put her pants, shirts, and underthings into the drawer. She looked down at the jewelry box, still hidden inside the suitcase, and then she snapped the suitcase shut and set it on the floor behind her bed.

"Well, if you're sure you can manage. . .you don't need anything. . ." Her aunt looked around the room anxiously. "Well. . .I best be helping Sally get dinner on. *God afton.*"

Kit smiled after her aunt. She wondered if her aunt sprinkled her speech at work with phrases from her first language. Kit could just picture her speaking Swedish to some executive.

Still smiling, Kit took out her Bible from the drawer

and put it on the nightstand between the two beds. She was about to sit down and open its pages, when Sally stuck her head in the door.

"Dearie, Clara is awake. She's asking for you."

five

*Bread of deceit is sweet to a man;
but afterwards his mouth shall be filled with gravel.*
Proverbs 20:17

❧

Keith Long registered for his conference at the tall, opulent convention center, and then he rented a car and made his way north to Anoka, a suburb of the Minneapolis-St. Paul metropolis. He hadn't seen his sister Beth since she had moved here with her husband and their two daughters, and he was anxious to visit their new home on the banks of the Mississippi River.

As he pulled the car up in front of the two-story house, its dark wood reminded him of a resort cottage he had stayed in once. A thought flashed through his mind, a vivid image of Kit's pleasure in this house, the light in her eyes as he took her boating on the river. He shook himself. Kit Anderson was unlikely to ever visit this house.

He turned off the ignition and swung his long legs out of the car. As he strode toward the house, however, he was still seeing wide blue eyes staring at him from between thick lashes.

❧

Kit's eyes closed for a quick prayer, and then she tiptoed across the hall to Gramma Clara's room. The last rays of the late afternoon sun made a shaft of hazy light around the bed. Within the sunlit bed, a fragile shape shifted slightly. Kit knew her grandmother watched her.

46

After a moment, a pale hand that was nearly transparent extended from the bed. "Kit. You gave me quite a shock." Clara's voice was soft but surprisingly strong. "For a second you took me back many many *aret*...years. Have you ever been told how much you look like your namesake, Katalina? Your blood grandmother—my best friend."

Kit shook her head. "Sally said I reminded her of Mom."

The old woman's eyes were tender. "*Ya*, you have Sophia's strength, I think, and her determination. Katalina was not physically strong. Slight she was and pretty, with a smile that warmed you like the sun. Like you."

"Gramma—" Kit shook her head again. "I'm not strong." She held her hands out, looked down at her legs. "I'm weak."

Clara reached for one of Kit's hands. "No. If you were not strong—both inside as well as out—you could not have gone through all that you have. You would have given up. No, you are strong...stronger, I fear, than I..." Her words trailed off.

"I don't understand."

Clara sighed. "You will, Katalina. You will." Her eyes clouded for a moment, as though she were seeing something long in the past, and then her attention snapped back to Kit. "*Var sa god och sitt ner*. Sit down, please, sit down."

Kit's legs had been aching, and now she thankfully pulled a vanity bench closer to the bed and sat on it. Clara smiled and gripped her hand, as though gathering strength from her.

"You have questions, *ya*?" she asked at last.

Kit nodded. "I don't understand why you wanted me to bring the jewelry box. Did you—did you think Mom should have left it to you?"

"*Ach*, no, Kit. It is yours and rightfully so. I just needed to see it, touch it, hold it once more before I die."

"I think maybe I understand," Kit said slowly. "When Mom died, I couldn't let go of the box. It seemed to give me comfort, knowing it was a piece of my heritage I could touch and hold, a symbol of my roots. But. . ."

"But what does that have to do with me, you are thinking, *ya*? Knew you not the box was once mine?"

Kit's eyes widened. "No!"

Clara's smile was soft and faraway. "How could you know? Let me tell you." For an instant she closed her eyes, and Kit could feel her sending her mind back in time. When her grandmother opened her eyes again, they were focused on the far wall, as though seeing something there invisible to Kit.

"I remember Katalina so well," Clara said. "Small, she was, pretty, always smiling. My best friend. Back in Sweden when we were young, we did everything together." Clara paused and her eyes turned toward Kit. "Do you know your grandmother's history?"

Kit shook her head, and her grandmother's eyes turned back to the wall. "Well, she was orphaned at seven, and then she was taken in and brought up by her uncle who was her godfather. He was the famous Swedish songwriter, A. L. Augustafson.

"He was already old when he took in his niece, and before long it was he who needed her to care for him. Not that she minded. He was very good to her always, and Katalina loved him like a father.

"But her constant care of her uncle angered my brother Edmund." Clara smiled and shook her head. "Back then, I thought certain my best friend would one day be my sister-in-law. You won't believe it now, but once Edmund was a tall lad, blond and handsome. His pride and joy was his long, bushy mustache." Clara laughed a little, remembering, and then her smile faded. "He demanded that Katalina spend more time with him. When she refused, he gave in and moved nearby to help her with the heavier tasks about the farm."

Kit leaned forward, fascinated, but her grandmother seemed unable to go on for a moment. When at last she did, her voice was hoarse with sadness. "Soon after, Katalina's uncle died, burned to death in a fire. It was Christmas, you see, and in those days before electricity, they'd lit the tree with candles. The tree caught fire and—" She shook her head. "Katalina and Ed were fortunate to escape alive. Afterward, the only thing left to Katalina was the jewelry box. She found it among the ruins, by some miracle perfectly intact.

"It was too much for poor Katalina. She had lost her parents at such a young age and now this. She ran away, away from the past, away from Ed, away to America to begin a new life.

"In Clayton, Wisconsin, she met Claus. He was older than her by ten years, but he was strong and capable, and he loved gentle Katalina. He was a good man, and Katalina married him. She wrote us of course, and I can still remember her letter, so full of love and hope. I was happy for her, but Edmund never understood. I had always thought, though, that my brother was too immature for Katalina, too full of boyish pranks for someone who had experienced so much pain."

Clara sighed and then continued. "I missed her, but I wished her well. And then word came my dear friend was . . ." the fingers that still gripped Kit's hand clutched tighter, "was dead. She died giving birth to your mother."

Kit swallowed. Her mother had never told her this story, only that her grandmother had died when she was very young. Sophia had never wanted to speak of the past, and Kit's persistent questions had been answered first with reluctance and then irritation. Her evasiveness had only increased Kit's curiosity about the past. Now at last she knew the truth.

"Claus deeply grieved for his young wife." Clara's voice had grown fainter, as though she were tiring. "One day he rented out his farm, packed up, and brought little Sophia to Sweden. He needed comforting, and his own family had died, and so he came looking for Katalina's people."

Clara smiled. "By this time, Edmund had joined the army and was far away, grieving in his own way, but Claus found me. In trying to ease each other's grief, we fell in love. Soon we married, and I became Sophia's mother. After a couple of years, we had Augusta. I was very happy."

Kit watched the memory of that happiness erase the lines of pain from Clara's face. "*Ya*," she continued, "that was a happy time. But Claus was restless for his farm back in America. Once again, he packed up, this time to return with his new family to America. I left my home in Sweden and I never returned. It did not matter to me. I had Claus."

She fell silent for a long moment. "The jewelry box, Gramma," Kit said at last. "What about it?"

"*Ya*, the box. Claus gave it to me, Katalina's box, for a wedding gift. He told me, 'Clara, have this. It is Katalina's love and Katalina's blessing. I want you to have it and so would she, I know. Only it must go to Sophia when she grows up.'

"So the box was mine. I gave it to your mother when she married." She shook her head. "So much has changed since those days. I never would have thought that Ed too would come to America. I never thought my Claus would die, leaving me alone with the farm and two young girls to raise. And then Sophia—I never would have thought I would live longer than my Sophia." Her voice broke. "It is past my time. I am ready to go. I want to see Katalina and Claus and Sophia."

Kit watched the tears that crept from beneath her grandmother's closed lids. "Shall I bring you the jewelry box now?" she asked gently.

Clara's eyes opened. She looked down at Kit's hand still clutched tight within her own, and with her other hand, she traced the gnarled lines of Kit's fingers. "*Ya*," she said finally. "I want to see the box once more. But child, I have no wish to bring my troubles upon you. You've been through so much already. . ."

"Trouble?" Kit frowned. "What trouble?"

Clara pushed her head forward off the pillow, as though trying to see Kit more clearly. "Are you happy?"

"Yes, Gramma," Kit answered automatically.

"Have you anyone to look out for you?"

Kit shrugged. "If you mean, did someone come with me to Minneapolis, then yes, Dr. Long, an associate of my orthopedist, traveled with me. He has a conference here in town this week."

"This man," Gramma's weak voice grew stronger and her eyes searched Kit's face, "he is special to you?"

Kit's cheeks grew warm. "No, Gramma. He's a kind man, a very kind man—but I only just met him. My doctor, Dr. Ellis, asked him to watch out for me. I don't think he really wanted to have me along."

The light drained from her grandmother's face, and she fell back against the pillow. "Oh." Her voice was only a whisper.

Sally stuck her head around the corner, then frowned and came into the room. She bent over Clara, then turned to Kit. "Maybe you better leave now, dearie. I'm afraid Clara has overexerted herself."

Kit nodded and moved to get up, but Clara tightened her grip on Kit's hand. "No, wait! What does it matter now if I tire myself? Kit will leave in a moment, Sally."

Sally hesitated. "Only a moment, then," she said and left them alone again.

Clara pulled Kit closer. "The jewelry box, Katalina. Have you told anyone about it?"

Kit shook her head. "No. Why?"

Clara pressed her lips together and shook her head. Her eyes drooped shut. "No time now. Promise me, though, you won't tell anyone else about it." Her lids opened and she fixed her eyes on Kit's face. "Promise me."

"I promise. But Aunt Augusta knows, you know. She was the one who told me to bring it."

"She's not the one who worries me. Just, just. . ." She seemed to be struggling for words.

Kit patted her hand. "Don't worry, Gramma. I won't show the box to anyone, or mention it either. You rest now."

Clara's face relaxed and her grip slackened. A moment later, her lids fell shut and her breathing slowed. Kit heard Sally enter the room, the nurse's solid shoes thudding quietly on the hardwood floor, and Kit got to her feet.

Sally put her finger on her lips, and Kit tiptoed from the room. She turned toward the living room, hesitated, and then went to her own room instead. She took off her pants and shirt, and belted on a white terry cloth robe.

In the bathroom, she quickly washed, then returned to

her room and slipped on the royal blue dress. She belted a wide black belt around her waist, and around her neck fastened a gold necklace that matched her bracelet. With her special comb, one that had been tacked onto a long polished stick, she smoothed her long hair.

For a moment she stared at herself in the mirror. She could do no better, she decided, and limped down the hall to the living room.

She found Lars still lounging on the sofa while he flipped idly through a magazine. Edmund was still hunched in the chair in the corner. Kit saw that he held an hourglass in his hand; as she watched, the sand ran out and he turned it over. The lamplight glowed on one side of his sunken face, leaving the other side in shadow, as though he were half demon, half angel. He leaned forward and set the hourglass on the end table beside his chair. Outside, the wind whipped through the juniper bushes, fluttering the curtains. Edmund picked up the hourglass and turned it over once more.

Kit shuddered. She turned to go back to her room to read until dinner, but she had hesitated too long. From the recesses of his chair, her great uncle whined, "Katalina. Come here."

Poor man, she thought, *sitting here day after day with nothing better to do than wait for his sister to die.* Her compassion pushed her forward into the living room.

She looked around the room, realizing that the large area rug was as rich a yellow as it was seven years ago when she last saw the room, the print covers on the chairs and sofas just as cheerful. When she had been here before, however, this room had been homey and welcoming, filled with contentment and laughter and peace. Now, it was dismal. Kit tried to decide what had changed.

The room's occupants, she realized. They were what made the room so different from the one she remembered, so filled with gloom.

She pulled the piano bench closer to Edmund's chair and sat next to him. "How are you, Uncle Edmund?"

"I am not so fine these days. Katalina, why do you come?"

"Gramma Clara asked for me."

Edmund's white brows raised. "Messing into things again, is she?" he muttered, his old voice harsh.

"What are you talking about, Uncle Edmund?"

He shook his head. "Nothing, nothing. Why did you come?" This time his voice was a whine again.

"Because Gramma Clara asked for me," Kit repeated.

"She does not need you. She has Augusta. She has me. She has. . .Lars."

Kit bit back a sarcastic reply about Lars' helpfulness to Gramma. Instead, she said mildly, "Gramma really wants my mother, I think. Since she can't have her, I'm the closest she can get."

The old man's mouth pulled tight in a bitter sneer. "Sophia was a capable one, always determined. Too stubborn, but she would have seen to things properly. What good are you?"

Kit bit her lip. Before she could think of an answer, Lars said, "You might as well go home, you know. You're in the way, if you want the truth. Sally has enough to take care of. Who needs you?"

Kit flushed, but to her surprise, Edmund said gruffly, "Don't mind the boy, Katalina. He never did know how to behave himself around a pretty girl." He gazed at Kit's face, and the hard lines of his features softened.

Lars stared deliberately at Kit's hands. "Pretty. Sure."

Kit closed her eyes. She crossed her arms and tucked her hands out of sight. "Maybe Aunt Augusta could use some help in the kitchen." She got to her feet and hurried as fast as she was able from the room.

The kitchen's warm smells and the welcoming smiles of Sally and Augusta eased Kit's tension. She watched as the two women pulled hot dishes from the stove and oven: tender roast, blueberry muffins, beans, piping hot potatoes. "May I help?" she asked.

Sally chuckled. "Dearie, this kitchen is a tight fit even for two people who are used to working together. We have dinner well in hand. You just go relax."

"Have you talked to Uncle Edmund yet?" Aunt Augusta asked.

"I just did." And she was not returning to the living room, Kit decided, even if the kitchen was off limits.

She could understand why Sally wouldn't want her help. At home, everything was arranged so she could reach it easily. But here. . . "Maybe I could set the table?"

Her aunt smiled. "Good idea. Sally, could you get Kit the dishes?"

"Here, dearie." The stout woman handed Kit a stack of china dinner plates. On top she piled the silverware, making a load so heavy Kit feared she would drop it. "Thanks," she said and staggered into the dining room.

Carefully, Kit avoided the many throw rugs. She edged around the crowded room, placing the dishes on the snowy linen table cloth. Her tongue caught between her lips in concentration, she limped down one side of the table, sidling past the tall cabinet that showed off the Sevres china and Dresden figurines, then up the table's other side, placing each setting carefully.

She gave a sigh of accomplishment just as Augusta

called, "Dinner!" Her aunt and Sally brought the steaming plates and bowls to the table from the kitchen. Uncle Edmund shuffled past, returning soon with a tie knotted around his neck and his thin hair combed.

Lars came to the table as he was, but Sally glared at him, and Augusta pleaded, "Please, Lars. At least go wash."

They sat down without him, leaving an empty chair beside Kit. When Lars returned, he stopped short and stared at the chair. "I'm not sitting by her."

"Lars!" gasped Augusta.

Sally heaved herself to her feet. "So sit here then. I'll be happy to sit next to Kit."

Kit stared down at her plate. "Uncle," she heard Augusta ask, "would you say grace?"

Kit looked up quickly and caught Lars' sneer before she closed her eyes. Her uncle muttered words Kit could not understand, and silently she said her own prayer. Then she reached eagerly for some of the delicious food.

"Uncle, what did you find to do today?" Augusta asked, her voice courteous.

Again Lars sneered. "What he usually does of course. Sit in that chair and rot."

Sally's eyes narrowed. "And what did *you* do today, Lars?"

"Well, I did go pick up my little crip of a gold-diggin' cousin."

Kit smiled at her cousin. His eyes shifted away from her uneasily.

Sally chuckled. "If I thought you were bright enough to listen, Lars, I'd suggest you be nice to your cousin." She met Lars' eyes meaningfully, and a strange tension stretched between them. The silence became uncomfortable.

"Did you know I was named for my grandmother, my real grandmother I mean?" Kit said brightly, trying to fill the silence. "Gramma was telling me about her this afternoon."

Four forks jerked to a halt. Sally smiled, her expression forced. "What did Clara tell you about her, dearie?"

Kit glanced at her uncle. "She told me you used to court Katalina, Uncle Edmund."

Edmund nodded, his thin lips tight.

"What happened?" Kit prodded. "Why didn't you go with her when she ran away to America?"

When his father made no answer, Lars rolled his eyes. "Well, Dad?"

"We were young." Edmund's pale cheeks grew red. "She never would listen to me. She ran out on—" He broke off and stabbed a piece of meat with his fork.

"But if you loved her," Kit asked, "couldn't you have followed her?"

"What good would that have done? By the time I knew where she was in America, she had married that old dirt farmer."

Augusta flushed. "Uncle," she said quietly, "my father was a prosperous and well-respected farmer."

Lars gave a bark of laughter. "I always thought Kat ran out because of the big fire. Right, Dad?"

Edmund's fist crashed onto the table. "Shut up!" He said something more in Swedish, too fast for Kit to follow.

The table was silent. Edmund picked up his fork again, but his hand shook so badly he dropped it with a clatter. Kit ate with her head bowed. Why had she opened her mouth? She glanced up and looked at the four faces around the table. Their expressions were all guarded; no one met anyone else's eyes. Something, Kit thought, was going on here that she didn't understand.

She sighed and wished for Keith Long's calm logic.

six

*. . .I have dreamed a dream,
and my spirit was troubled to know the dream.*
Daniel 2:3

❧

The hostility that crackled around the table made Kit feel even more small and vulnerable than usual. If only she had not delved into the past—and yet she wanted to know more. Why all the secrecy? Why the hostility. . .and fear?

She tried to break the tension with an innocent question. "Uncle Edmund, when did you first come to America?"

"Forty-four," Edmund frowned, "no, forty-three years ago. I immigrated the year after Claus died." He glanced quickly at Augusta. Kit's aunt fingered the stem of her glass, her face pale. Edmund straightened his thin shoulders. "Yes, that was when I came over. You remember, don't you, Augusta? Or maybe you wouldn't."

Lars grunted and rolled his eyes. "Not too likely she would, is it?"

"Why?" Kit asked. "How old were you when Uncle Edmund came, Aunt Augusta?"

Augusta looked down at her ice cream. "Fifteen," she said quietly.

"Fifteen. And you don't remember?"

Sally patted Kit's hand, the touch almost a slap, her mouth tight. "Dearie," she said, "your aunt was in the hospital at the time."

Kit choked on a spoonful of ice cream. "I'm sorry," she said. "I didn't know."

Lars grinned. "Just another of the family skeletons, right, Augusta?"

Augusta set down her spoon. "Kit is family. We have no need to keep secrets from her." She took a deep breath and turned toward her niece. "At the time, Kit, I was in a sanitarium. You see after Dad—passed away, I had a . . .nervous breakdown, I guess you'd call it." Her lips twitched as though she were trying to smile. Very carefully, she picked her spoon up and then set it down again. She touched her napkin to her mouth, and then continued. "After I was released, neither Sophia nor Mama would ever let anyone talk about it. They were protecting me, because. . .because I was so embarrassed about it."

Sally turned toward Kit also, her face smiling once again. "Augusta doesn't remember much of anything that went on that year or so after her father's death."

"Because she was in the loony bin," put in Lars.

"Sanitarium," Sally corrected firmly. "She has no recollection of the night her father died."

At the word "died," Kit saw her aunt clench her fists, and her face tightened as though she were in pain.

"Water under the bridge," Edmund said. "Doesn't matter now. Leave your aunt alone, Katalina. Some things are best forgotten." Although he spoke to Kit, his eyes were fastened on Augusta. He looked more alert than Kit had yet seen him, though his face was filled with sadness.

Kit looked from Edmund's face to her aunt's. *Forgetting the past hasn't worked for Aunt Augusta,* she thought. *Her life has been built on that hidden fear and pain. Wouldn't she be better off if she brought her fear out into the light? Then maybe she could be free of it at last.*

She opened her mouth, but before she could speak, her aunt said quickly, "That roast was delicious, Sally."

Lars leaned back and patted his paunch. "I'm stuffed. Great cookin', Sally." He pulled out a cigar and lit up.

"Please, Lars," Augusta protested. "Think of Mother. It's not good for her lungs. You know we don't let anyone smoke in this house."

"Augusta's right." Sally scowled at Lars. "Any smoke in the air makes it harder for Clara to breathe."

Lars exchanged a look with the nurse, his eyes narrowed. "So? The quicker she goes the better, so far as I'm concerned."

Augusta gasped. "Lars!" She turned to her uncle. "Uncle Edmund, please."

Edmund shrugged and lurched to his feet, and Kit noticed that once again his eyes were vague, his face slack. Ignoring his son, he hobbled back to his place in the living room. Kit shook her head and left Lars and his cigar smoke alone at the table.

She found Augusta crying into the dishwater.

"Aunt Augusta, what's wrong?"

Her aunt wiped her hands on a dish towel, then took an embroidered handkerchief from her apron pocket and blew her nose. "I'm all right. Really I am."

Kit hesitated. "If you're sure." She went to help Sally clear the table.

While Sally checked on Clara, Kit helped her aunt with the dishes. "Lars is awfully rude," she said, drying a plate.

Her aunt made a face. "I never could get along with him, even when we were younger. He was much younger than I, of course, but even as a boy he was too lazy, too mischievous, . . .too violent."

Kit set the plate carefully on the counter and reached

for another. "Do you have to put up with him being here all the time?"

Her aunt shrugged. "Maybe after Mother passes on and the estate is settled. . .I'm hoping he'll leave by himself. If he doesn't. . .I don't know. He is my cousin."

Kit's lips tightened. "Not a very nice one."

"I know. I'm sorry, Kit, to have pulled you into all this. So much is happening right now. Maybe I shouldn't have asked you to come. Maybe I did the wrong thing. . .I just don't know. . . ." Her voice cracked, as though new tears threatened to overwhelm her, and her shoulders slumped.

They finished the dishes in silence, and Kit went to her bedroom to read.

She had left the mystery she'd brought in the suitcase, she remembered, and pulled the case onto the bed. She unsnapped the locks, then stared down into the case. The book was there—but the jewelry box was gone!

Who could have taken it? Besides her grandmother and aunt, who even knew she had the box with her? And why would someone take it anyway? It had sentimental value, and it probably had some value as an antique—but Gramma had lots of more valuable antiques in plain sight. Why take this one?

Kit wished she could run to tell her grandmother what had happened, but she knew she should not worry her. She could tell Aunt Augusta—but her aunt seemed to already have too much on her mind. Besides, what could she do?

Kit sat down and opened her book, but over and over she read the same two pages without even realizing. The room grew dark, and she switched on the lamp, then turned back to the book. She hadn't understood more than a sentence or two, though, even after reading for several minutes, and at last she slapped the book shut. She reached instead for her Bible.

Just holding the worn book comforted her, even if she couldn't concentrate on the words, but the missing jewelry box continued to occupy her mind. She wondered if she could search the house after everyone else was in bed. She shook her head. Unless the box was somewhere in plain sight, she wasn't likely to find it. After all, she wasn't able to climb on top of chairs or crawl on the floor searching for hiding places.

She sighed and stood up. She might as well go to bed. In the morning, things might look better.

As she unbuckled her belt, a knock at the door startled her. "Hey," Lars yelled. "Telephone for ya."

Gladness welled up in her as she refastened her belt with trembling fingers, and she hurried to the phone. Who knew to reach her here except for—? She picked up the receiver. "Hello?"

"Kit. This is Dr. Long. . .Keith." His deep voice sounded oddly tentative.

Joy washed over her in a wave so strong that she reached for a chair to steady herself. "Kei—" She glanced at the listening faces turned toward her in the living room, and said quickly, "Dr. Long. I'm so glad to hear from you."

Keith heard the happiness in her voice, but beneath it, he thought he also heard a note of anxiety, as though she had been recently upset. He shook his head at this new sensitivity of his, but he couldn't keep himself from asking, "Are you all right?"

He was certain she hesitated for longer than necessary. "I arrived safely," she said at last, as though she were struggling to be both positive and honest.

"How is your grandmother?"

"Everyone tells me it's just a matter of time."

Keith frowned. Why did he hear that note of fear in her voice?

Kit gripped the receiver tighter, afraid Keith would become bored with her stumbling and hesitation. She didn't want him to hang up. Hearing his voice was like a lifeline back to the normal world. That alone was reason enough to explain the joy that filled her, she told herself. Wanting to hang onto him a little longer, she said quickly, "How is your sister and her family?"

Why is her voice so breathless? Keith asked himself silently. When he spoke, he made his own voice slow and calm, trying between his words to send her a message of comfort and strength. "They're fine. I wish you could meet them, Kit. I know my sister Beth would like you." He should bring the conversation to a close now, he thought, but he found himself describing the house in detail, then telling her about his niece's small puppy that had nipped his ankle. Kit giggled, and he thought he could sense her relaxing on the other end of the line.

"That's better," he said softly. "Feeling better now?"

"Yes." Her eyes burned at the gentleness of his voice.

"I wish you would tell me what's bothering you."

Kit hesitated. "I'd like to. But. . .I can't. . .right now."

"You're not alone?"

"That's right."

Frustrated, Keith pressed his lips together. But why should he feel such a need to know what was bothering her? The only reason he had called her was because he had promised Ken Ellis he would check on her. Wasn't it? So he had done that, and now it was time to say goodbye. But those blue eyes of hers were still haunting him, and he sensed her desperate need to confide in him. Well, he had promised to watch out for her. Perhaps as part of his Christian duty, he should. . . "Look, Kit, do you have plans for tomorrow?"

"No." Her heartbeat quickened. "Not really. Why?"

"How would you like to come out here and meet Beth? Have dinner here?" He drawled the invitation coolly, bracing himself for a flirtatious response.

"Could I?" The frankness of her voice surprised him, and he was forced to laugh at himself.

At the note of genuine pleasure in his laugh, his sister, watching television across the room from him, glanced up. She looked at her brother curiously. His usually solemn face was lit, she saw, and she wondered who was bringing that expression to his eyes.

"Let me ask my sister," she heard him say, and he turned toward her. "Beth, may I bring a guest over for lunch tomorrow?"

Beth smiled, pleased that her curiosity would soon be satisfied. "Of course," she answered. "But what about your conference?"

Kit echoed the question on the phone. "Won't that interfere with your conference?"

Keith smiled. "Don't worry. The afternoon session is a boring one I can well afford to miss. I'll pick you up about eleven."

After he had hung up, he turned toward his sister, still smiling. She raised her eyebrows at him. "So who is this woman you're trying to impress?"

His smile disappeared. "She's not—I'm not trying to impress anyone. I'm concerned about her, that's all. I thought she might need to get away for a while. Kit would enjoy a picnic on the terrace."

"Kit? You mean the young handicapped woman you

traveled with?"

"Yes." He picked up a folder and stood up, ending the conversation. "I think I'll go to my room. I have some things I want to look over before tomorrow."

Beth watched him go, a musing light in her brown eyes.

⋙

Kit stood for a moment longer, her hand still on the phone, as though that could prolong her contact with Keith. Edmund's whine interrupted her. "Another beau, Katalina?" Kit was sure she heard a note of jealousy in his voice.

But that made no sense. She swung around to face him, almost losing her balance. "What did you say, Uncle Edmund?"

Lars laughed. "He's out of it right now. Thinks you're the other Katalina—his long lost love."

Kit watched as her uncle seemed to shrink in on himself. "No," she said gently, "no beau. Just a friend, Uncle Edmund."

She hurried back to her bedroom, feeling Lars' eyes on her like a cold hand between her shoulder blades. *Where are Aunt Augusta and Sally?* she wondered. Panic rippled inside her, like cold water drowning the warm glow Keith's voice had given her, and she scolded herself for being as hysterical as the heroine of her mystery novel.

Quickly, she slipped out of her dress and pulled a long lace-trimmed nightgown over her head. She belted on her robe and made a quick trip to the bathroom, then returned to the bedroom and sank down on her bed. She was exhausted, not only physically but mentally and spiritually as well, and she reached automatically for her Bible.

She turned to Ephesians 6: "Finally, my brethren, be strong in the Lord, and in the power of his might." She read the chapter to its end, then read it over yet again, more slowly this time, savoring each word like the spiritual food it was.

Her anxiety and confusion faded from her mind, and comfort and strength filled her. In this strange situation, she had felt even weaker than usual—but God had promised to give her strength, all the strength she needed for the task He had set before her.

But just what was that task? Discouragement flooded through her once again. She sensed such fear in them all, her aunt, her uncle, even Sally and Lars. Even Gramma, who had always before seemed so calm and serene, so sure of herself. . .like Kit's own mother. *If only,* thought Kit, *if only Mama were here. . .*

"Why did you take Mama away, God?" she whispered. "I need her. Gramma needs her. I don't understand what's going on here. What can I do?" She felt washed under by a sudden surge of fear and self-doubt, a cold, sinking feeling that left her certain that God found her just as repulsive as Lars did. She had failed God before, or He would have healed her completely.

Despite her despair, she forced herself to continue praying. "Help me, God. Please help me. I don't know where else to turn. I feel so alone. . ."

Almost at once, as warm as sunlight, the image of Keith Long poured into her mind. Against her closed lids, she could clearly see his tall legs, his long arms that had held her so securely, the enigmatic face, the calm, logical voice. Somehow, he seemed closer to her now than any of her relatives. And tomorrow she would see him, tomorrow she could ask his advice.

Not bothering to explain to herself why the thought of the psychiatrist should bring her such comfort, she slipped under the bed cover. "Thank You, Lord," she breathed. A few moments later she was asleep, a smile on her lips.

&

As Augusta got ready for bed, she saw the smile still lingering there. She looked at her sleeping niece for a moment, and wondered what had put the look of happiness on her face. Augusta moved quietly about the room, careful not to disturb Kit, envying her niece's peaceful sleep. Augusta couldn't remember her sleep ever being as deep and free of worry as Kit's seemed to be. For years, Augusta had avoided sleep like an enemy—but of course eventually she had to go to bed. She pulled a bottle out of a drawer and shook a pill into her hand, then gulped it down.

&

Kit jerked awake. She flung back the covers and sat up. What had she heard? Her eyes searched the darkness, her ears strained. . .nothing. Silence. But she had heard something. A scream, she thought. Perhaps it had only been a dream.

She started to lie down again, when she heard her aunt shift in the other bed. "I did it," she moaned. "I did it. I did it. I did it."

Kit reached over and gently shook her aunt's shoulder. "Aunt Augusta, you're dreaming. Are you all right? I think you screamed."

The older woman sat up and sighed. "Thank goodness. Just a dream." In the dim light from the hallway, Kit saw her rub her gaunt face.

"Not just a dream," Kit said. "You mean a nightmare. From the sounds of it, it must have been a bad one."

"*Ach, ya,* a nightmare." Augusta suddenly pushed back the covers and scrambled to her feet. "Mother! I hope I didn't wake her. I think I should check. But then, what if I didn't wake her before, but I do wake her by checking on her? Oh, I don't know. What do you think?" She turned toward Kit.

"Shh." Kit listened to the silent house. "I don't hear anything. I think she must have slept through it."

"If you're sure?" Augusta lay back down. For a moment she was silent; Kit could hear the quick in and out of her breathing. After a moment she said, "I don't think . . .I don't think I'll be able to sleep again now."

"I'm wide awake too," Kit said. "Maybe you'd feel better if you told me about the nightmare."

"*Ya*, maybe," Augusta said softly. She hesitated, then sighed. "So bright, it was. I was young and happy. Under a tall, thick oak tree, I was playing, playing with my favorite dolls, I can still see them. . . Papa had built me a little doll house there, and I always used to play. . . But in the nightmare," Augusta's voice changed, filled with fear, "suddenly the tree fell. My little house was smashed to pieces. And Papa was there, lying on the ground. Beside him was something long and cold and slimy. It looked like yarn, like yellow yarn, like my doll's hair, only it wasn't, it was something else. . . For a long time, I stared and stared at it. And then—then I could feel myself falling into pieces, just like the doll house had. I think that's when I screamed."

Kit looked at her through the shadows. "Sounds pretty awful. Have you any idea what gave you the nightmare? Did something like that ever happen to you?"

Her aunt shook her head. "No. Of course not. I'm sure . . .I'm sure it has to do with Dad's. . .passing." She was quiet for a long moment and when she spoke again, her voice shook. "I'm afraid they're coming back."

"What are? What are coming back, Aunt Augusta?"

"My nightmares." Kit saw a shudder shake her aunt's thin body.

"You've had nightmares like this before?"

"*Ya*. After. . .after. . ."

"After your father died," Kit finished quietly.

"*Ach, ya*. But it has been such a long time now. They were bad at first, I remember that, real bad. . . But they went away. The people at that place, they helped me."

"And you haven't had the nightmares since then? Not until now?"

Her aunt shook her head. "Nothing like tonight. Oh, I don't sleep well, I never have. I have to take something . . .but tonight. . .oh, I don't know what to do! What am I to do, child?" She turned toward her niece, and Kit saw the fear in her face. "Is this the beginning of it again? Will they have to send me away again?"

"You only had a nightmare, Aunt Augusta," Kit said gently. "That doesn't mean you'll have a nervous breakdown again. Probably the things we talked about at dinner brought it on. Or maybe just the stress of Gramma being so sick."

"Are you sure?" Kit heard her aunt's desperate need for reassurance.

"I'm sure."

Augusta gave a deep sigh. She sat up and swung her legs out of bed. "You're probably right, Kit. I think I'll go check on Mother now, just to be sure she's sleeping and doesn't need anything. Just to put my own mind at rest." She pulled on a long robe. "And then I'm going to fix myself some hot milk. Want to join me?"

Kit hesitated. Her aunt's lips twitched nervously. "Oh, I'm sorry. You don't like hot milk, probably. Well, you needn't have it hot, of course. Or I could make you some tea. Whatever. . ."

Kit smiled. "Sure, Aunt Augusta. I'll join you in the kitchen."

❧

Thankfully, the hot milk did calm her aunt and they returned to their beds. Only a moment later, Kit thought, the smell of bacon and eggs woke her. With a groan, she forced her eyes open, then slid out from the covers and headed for the bathroom.

After a quick shower, she dressed in white pants and a white silk blouse she left open at the neck. She slid a headband over her damp hair, a black one to match her belt and shoes. She added a touch of blush to her pale cheeks, then stared at her reflection in the mirror, frowning. After a moment, she touched her lips with a burgundy lipstick. She smiled at the result.

Still smiling, she went to the dining room, where her aunt was just finishing a cup of coffee, an empty plate in front of her.

"Good morning, Aunt Augusta." Kit sat down across from her aunt, hiding a yawn as Sally brought her a plate full of bacon and eggs.

Edmund came into the room and caught her with her hand over her mouth. "Bad night, Katalina? Couldn't sleep?"

Kit shook her head. "I fell asleep easily enough. Both when I went to bed and after Aunt Augusta woke me up." She blinked, realizing she had made a mistake.

Wearing baggy tan pants and a wrinkled black and white T-shirt, Lars leaned against the doorway. "So cousin woke you up, did she? How strange."

Kit shrugged, stifling another yawn. "She just had a

bad dream."

Edmund turned toward Augusta. "A nightmare?"

Augusta frowned. "I. . .I suppose it was." She looked into her coffee cup, then threw Kit a pleading glance. "Kit said it was just due to the talk last night. And the stress . . . Please, it was nothing. Forget it. I. . .I'm fine."

Lars' lips twisted. "You better be, cousin. We wouldn't want no repeat performances, you going loony tunes like you did when you were young."

Augusta's already pale face lost all trace of color. Her hand gripped the coffee cup with white knuckles, until Kit thought surely the cup would shatter. Her aunt opened her mouth—but at that moment, Sally bustled in again, a large glass of milk for Kit in her hand.

"Good morning, Lars," Sally said. "Sit down and I'll get you a plate."

"How's Gramma this morning?" Kit asked.

"I think she's still sleeping," Augusta answered. "She seems to be still as peaceful as when I checked on her around two."

"After your nightmare?" Sally asked. She ignored Augusta's flush, and said, "There's no need to worry about Clara's sleep at this point. You'll find she sleeps more and more these days, and there's nothing that's going to disturb her. It's you I'm worried about, Augusta. You can't let yourself become overwrought, you know. Tonight I insist you take those pills I brought you. Those ones you're taking obviously aren't doing the job."

"Have you checked with her doctor?" Kit didn't like the idea of her aunt taking pills to sleep.

"I'm sure it's all right," Augusta assured her niece. "After all, Sally is a nurse. If she thinks the pills will help. . . Of course, the dream really was nothing. I don't know why you're all making such a fuss. It was nothing. . ."

"That's not what Pop thinks, is it, Pop?" taunted Lars.

Sally turned to the shrunken old man. "So just what is it that you do think?"

"Ask her." Edmund nodded his head toward Augusta. "Sounds to me like the nightmares she had when she went over the edge."

"Nonsense." Kit's voice was exasperated. "Aunt Augusta, don't listen to this silly talk. I'm sorry I ever said anything about your bad dream."

"It's all right, Kit." Her aunt sighed, her shoulders slumped. She pushed back her chair and got slowly to her feet, her back bent like an old woman's. "I have to get ready for work now."

Kit went to the kitchen to help Sally clean away the breakfast things. A few minutes later, when Augusta came through the kitchen on her way out the door, Kit was surprised to see that her aunt's shoulders were once more straight, her step brisk. The hesitant old woman was gone, replaced by the purposeful businesswoman.

After Augusta was gone, Sally went to tend Clara, and Kit headed for her own room to read. After a short time, however, she thought she heard Sally call her.

Kit went across the hall and stuck her head in her grandmother's room. "Did you want me?"

Sally turned from the old woman's bed. "Yes, dearie, your grandmother would like to talk to you. Try not to let her get overtired, though."

"I'll try not to." Kit limped across the room and pulled a seat near to the bed.

"Kit." Her grandmother's voice was faint.

"I'm here, Gramma."

"I overheard some talk of nightmares. Did Augusta

have one?"

Kit hesitated. "There was some talk at the table last night," she said finally. "About the past."

Clara reached for Kit's hand. "Tell me about her nightmare. What did she dream?"

"Well. . .she said it was like the ones she had after her father died. But surely that's understandable. Uncle Edmund thought—"

Her grandmother's fingers tightened painfully. "Edmund knows she had a nightmare?"

"Yes, we talked about it at breakfast."

Clara's eyes dropped shut and she fell back against the pillow. "Last night at the table—you talked about Claus, *ya*? About his death?"

"We did. I didn't realize until too late how much the talk would hurt Aunt Augusta. After all, it was so many years ago."

"*Ach*, Kit, you don't understand." The old woman's hands plucked at her covers. "It is dangerous for Augusta to have those nightmares. It is dangerous for her to remember too much."

Kit put a soothing hand on her grandmother's arm, trying to calm her. "I know about Aunt Augusta's breakdown. But that was so long ago too. Surely it would be good for Aunt Augusta to accept the past, to stop fearing it so much."

Clara shook her head. "You don't understand," she repeated. "You must not make Augusta have these nightmares. You must not dig up the past." Her faded eyes held Kit's. "I know you are curious about the past. That is only natural. But let me answer your questions. You want to know about your grandfather? I will tell you anything you want to know about Claus. What do you want to know?"

"I don't want to tire you."

"Nonsense. I'll talk as much as I like. It's about the only thing left I *can* do. You of all people should understand. Just because you and I may not be able to get around the same way others can, doesn't mean they can tell us not to talk." The old woman smiled. "I am right, *ya*?"

Kit grinned. "*Ya*, Gramma, you are right. I'll stay as long as you want to talk." Her smile faded. "Could you tell me how my grandfather died, Gramma?"

Once more Clara closed her eyes. "Claus had a heart condition. One night he asked Augusta to bring his pills. He felt an attack coming on, you see—but by the time she brought the pills, it was too late. Claus—" Clara's voice broke, "Claus was gone. Augusta blamed herself. It was not her fault, of course, but no one could convince her. She told you what happened to her afterward?"

"She had a nervous breakdown."

"*Ya*, she did not come out of it for over a year."

"And she still can't remember what happened that night?"

Clara shook her head. "Somewhere in here," she pointed to her temple, "I believe she knows. But if she tries too hard to remember, it may be bad for her. I'm afraid. . ."

"Afraid of what, Gramma?"

Clara turned her head away. "Now I am too tired to talk more, Kit. Will you do one last thing for me?"

"If I can."

"Go upstairs and bring down the photo albums, the old ones with Claus in them. I would like to look at his face."

"Sure, Gramma. I'll go right now." But Gramma Clara was asleep before Kit left the room. As she tiptoed out, she remembered the jewelry box. *I'll tell her later,* she thought, and opened the door to the stairway.

She stared in dismay. The stairs were steep, with no railing. Why couldn't Gramma have asked Sally or Augusta to fetch the albums? Kit hesitated, tempted to ask Sally for help. But no, Gramma knew what the stairs were like and still she had asked Kit; she must have had her reasons.

Kit carefully tested each step, one at a time, her hand on the wall for balance. At last, breathing heavily, she reached the floor above.

The unfinished upstairs was as neat as the floor below, boxes neatly shelved, without a sign of dust or cobwebs, testimony to Aunt Augusta's craving for perfection. On a shelf in the corner, Kit found the albums.

Not eager to make the climb downstairs with the heavy albums clutched under her arm, she stood for a moment, thumbing through the yellowed pages. She saw pictures of her grandmother Katalina, her grandfather, a young and pretty Augusta.

One picture caught her eye. In it her aunt stood beside a handsome young man, handsome except for the familiar twist of his lips.

seven

Every purpose is established by counsel. . . .
Proverbs 20:18a

≈

Lars? Kit stared at the picture. She shook her head. Lars was much younger than Aunt Augusta; the man in the picture could not be him.

"Kit," called Sally's voice up the stairwell. "Have you found those albums Clara's wanting?"

"Yes," Kit called back. "Be right down."

She slammed the album closed and tucked it under her arm with two of the other fat books. Slowly, carefully, she went down the steep stairs, afraid she would lose her balance and pitch forward. When she reached the bottom at last, she sighed. "Lord," she said under her breath, "I'd really rather not have to go up or down those stairs again."

As soon as she had caught her breath, she took the albums to her grandmother. "How are you feeling?"

Clara shrugged. "The same. Just a little tired. You have found the pictures, *ya?*"

Kit laid them on her grandmother's lap. Clara opened the top album, then ran her hand across the picture inside, caressing the long-ago face. "Look, Kit. Here is my Claus. Was he not handsome? See, here is our wedding picture. Don't we look solemn?" One by one, Clara pored over the pictures. "We were so happy then, before. . ."

"Before he died?"

Clara jumped, as though she had forgotten Kit's

77

presence. "*Ya*," she said quickly. "*Ya*, of course, before he died." She leaned back against the pillow, her breath trembling.

"Are you all right? Do you want me to call Sally?"

Clara shook her head. "No, dear. Not yet. I'm just feeling. . .sorry for things that happened in the past. An old woman's regrets." She looked up at Kit. "Have you ever done anything you wish you could undo?"

"Of course." Kit shifted her weight, her legs aching. "Who hasn't?"

"*Ya*, but for me. . . I am going to die soon." Clara's voice was soft. "I would like to. . .make amends. But perhaps it is too late. If only you were not involved, Sophia . . ."

Kit stepped closer to the bed. "Gramma, is there something I could do? Like Mom would do, if she could be here. You did ask me to come. Let me help you."

Clara's eyes fastened on Kit's face. "Perhaps. You are much like your mother. You have her inner peace, her strength of character. I wish Augusta. . ." She shook her head. "Go now. I am too tired to think what I should do. We will talk again later."

"What about the albums?"

Her grandmother clutched them against her chest. "Leave them here." Her eyes sank shut. "Claus. . ."

Kit tiptoed from the room. She found Sally in the dining room setting the table for lunch. "Here," Kit said, reaching for the plates, "let me help. I forgot to tell you at breakfast, though—I won't be here for lunch."

Sally looked at her. "Oh?"

"A. . .a friend is picking me up." Kit felt her cheeks grow warm.

"How nice. I had no idea you had friends here in the

city. Someone you met when you were at the rehabilitation center here?"

"No. No, he traveled here with me. He's attending a conference here."

"Oh." Again she threw a look at Kit.

"I'm sorry. I should have told you this morning. My mind's been on Gramma, I guess."

Sally handed Kit the silverware. "Speaking of Clara, I'd better check on her. I'll let you finish here."

She returned a few minutes later. "Here," she said, handing Kit the stack of albums. "You left these on Clara's bed."

"She wouldn't let me take them. She wanted to look at Claus, she said. I think she's longing to be with him again."

"Aye, dearie." Sally picked up one of the albums and leafed through it. "We can't be sad for her, though. She's had a long, full life."

"I know." Kit blinked away tears. "But even though I know she'll be with Claus, with my mother—I'll still miss her." She gripped the back of a dining room chair, hating to think that soon she would lose still another person she loved.

Sally smiled. "You're religious too, I can see, dearie. That's good if it gives you comfort."

Kit searched the nurse's face. "You talk as though you don't believe it yourself."

The other woman shrugged. "Death is death, so far as I'm concerned. The time to live is here, now. That's why I believe we have to grab all the happiness we can while we have the chance."

Kit shook her head. "I don't believe life ends with death. But I agree that in the meantime we should live each moment to the fullest. Jesus promised not only some far-off paradise, but peace and strength for each day." She longed to convince Sally, but her own heart accused her. Did she herself really have any more faith in God than Sally did? God was the One who had taken her parents from her. God was the One who had failed to heal her completely.

Sally looked at Kit's face, and her eyebrows rose. "You really believe this yourself? After all you've been through, you really believe God cares for you?"

"I have a lot of doubts sometimes," Kit admitted. "I don't always understand. . .but yes, I do believe." She turned toward the table to align a fork beside a plate, afraid her face would show how great her doubts were.

Sally shrugged. "Fine for you, I guess. Mind if we change the subject?"

"Where's Lars?" Kit asked obligingly. "Don't tell me he and Edmund left?"

Sally shook her head. "Edmund's right there in his spot in the living room, turning that hourglass over and over. Gets on my nerves, let me tell you. Hard to see him now as the debonair man I once knew."

"Clara says he was quite handsome."

Sally sniffed. "He was also bullheaded, stubborn as a mule, and always getting in trouble." Her eyes flashed. "His sister was always having to rescue him."

"You sound as though you knew him from way back."

Sally shrugged. "I grew up around here. My folks were the outsiders in an otherwise Swedish settlement. Made it hard sometimes, specially since the Swedes really believed theirs was the language of heaven." She laughed, but Kit heard a note of bitterness in her voice.

"Clara was always nice to me, though. She let me earn money by helping around the house when I was a girl. So yes, I've been around this family for a while. I knew a lot of what went on."

"Then you were around when Edmund came over from America?" Kit leaned forward.

Sally glanced away. "That's right. I went with the family when they picked him up. I was a girl at the time, a teenager." She hesitated. "Edmund tried to settle down. He married and had Lars—and then woke up one morning when Lars was scarcely out of diapers and found his wife gone, took off with some other man. Edmund wasn't particularly good with kids, and I used to help out with Lars."

"And yet you don't like either of them very much, do you?"

Sally's heavy shoulders lifted, and she made a face. "I know them too well. They're stubborn and not too bright. They can be led, though, all too easily." She shook her head. "That Edmund. He never was much of a man, for all his handsome looks, and now Lars is even worse."

"You knew Edmund pretty well, sounds like."

"I should. I was in his house often enough taking care of the two of them. For a while, he and I even thought of making our arrangement permanent."

"You and Uncle Edmund?"

Sally laughed. "Hard to believe, huh? But this was a long time ago, remember. He wasn't so bad then." She slapped the album shut and shuffled her bulk into the kitchen.

Kit knew she would get no more out of Sally today. Thoughtfully, she went to her room to freshen her makeup, then sat down in the living room to wait for Keith.

She avoided looking at either her uncle or Lars, but from the corner of her eye she could see Edmund turning and turning the hourglass. Lars, she knew, was watching her, his face twisted in its usual sneer. She sat on the edge of her chair, watching the clock, and breathed a sigh of relief when she heard a knock at the door.

Neither Edmund nor Lars made any move to answer the door, and, as fast as she was able, Kit rushed to open it. "Dr. Long." She stared up at him, noticing all over again the size of him, the dark hair that fell across his forehead, his gray eyes that gave away no hint of his feelings. Relief washed over her, and she swayed against the door frame.

Keith reached for her arm. "Are you all right?" He felt her tremble beneath his hand and frowned. "What is it?"

She smiled. "It's nothing. I'm fine. Please. . .come in and meet. . .everyone."

Keith followed her inside, noting with interest the faces of the two men who sat in the dark room. Edmund roused himself only enough to ask, "Doctor?"

Lars laughed. "Checking up on your patient, are you? Didn't know her condition was so bad she needed house calls."

"I'm a psychiatrist, not an orthopedist," Keith answered coolly.

Lars' brows raised. "So, Kit, you're as crazy as cousin Augusta?"

Kit bit her lip, embarrassed by her relations, but she felt Keith's warm hand against the small of her back, comforting her even as it sent strange tingles through her body. "I'm a friend of Kit's," he said easily. "That's all."

Lars shrugged. Edmund turned the hourglass over and stared into its depths. Kit could feel the fear and tension and hate coiling in the room, and unconsciously she took a step nearer to Keith, looking up into his face.

"I'm glad to have met you both," Keith said, "but we

must be going. Ready, Kit?"

"Oh, yes." She sighed with relief and reached for her purse. "I'm ready."

Keith hurried her out of the shadowed house and into his car. His lips tightened; after what he had just seen of her family, he intended to make sure Kit enjoyed herself this afternoon.

He drove silently, frowning a little. As her grandmother's house fell further and further behind, he saw Kit relax. She lay her head back against the head rest, and her hands unclenched in her lap.

"Been pretty awful?"

She nodded. "I wasn't prepared for it to be so bad. The last time I was here, back when I was at Sister Kenny Rehab seven years ago, things were nothing like this." She took a deep breath. "Thanks."

He smiled. "For what?"

"For getting me out of there."

"My pleasure."

They fell silent again, until at last Kit stirred and looked out her window. "Where are we headed?"

"Anoka."

"That's quite a ways, isn't it?"

"Thirty miles or so. Beth has a new house on the Mississippi. Wait till you see it. You'll love it."

"You're sure your sister doesn't mind my coming?"

He shook his head. "No. She's much more. . .outgoing than I am. Likes to meet new people."

Kit watched as the tall buildings gave place to long flat ones, then houses, then a stretch of countryside that reminded her of home. She found herself thinking of her conversation earlier with Sally, wishing she was as sure of her faith as she had tried to sound.

"Dr. Long?" she said hesitantly.

"It's Keith, remember?" He gave her a sidelong smile. "What is it?"

"I—I was talking with Sally earlier—she's Gramma's nurse, an old friend of the family—and she was questioning my belief that God loves and cares for us. I tried to sound confident about my own faith. . .I wanted to convince her. . .but, truthfully. . .well, sometimes I'm not so sure God really does care about me." She looked down at her hands. "Lars treats me like I'm a leper. I know God wouldn't care about that, about my physical condition, but sometimes I think He must feel about me the same way as Lars does, repulsed. . . I think maybe I've done something so awful He can't love me. Why else would He take away both my mother and father? Why would He leave me like this?" She held her hands up in the air.

Keith opened his mouth to speak, but when he glanced at Kit, he saw she had still more she needed to say. He drove silently, listening.

"I wanted so badly to go out on a date when I was in college." Now that she had started, years of hurt and pain were tumbling out of her. "Oh, I had some friends. But the young men either treated me like a sister—someone to listen to their affairs and give advice—or else they thought I was a child to play with, to cosset and look out for. And then there were others who. . ."

"Who rejected you because of your handicap."

Kit nodded, staring blindly out the window. "I think I must have failed God somehow. . .but sometimes I get so . . .so mad at Him for failing *me*. I love Him, I truly do. I want to serve Him, but. . ." She fell silent, gulping back tears. Why had she said so much? What would Keith think of her?

He reached over and squeezed her arm. "So you've been afraid to love or trust—not only God, but anyone else either."

Kit turned to look at him. "How did you know that?"

"Your feelings aren't unusual, Kit." He considered his words carefully. "Tell me," he said at last, "what horrible thing have you done to make God turn His back on you?"

"That's just it. I don't know. I've thought and thought about it but. . ."

"Do you know that verse about Satan being the accuser of the brethren?"

"Yes."

"Well, Kit, I think you've been listening to the accuser's voice—not God's. You've let yourself be filled with doubt because you're hurt, and you don't understand how a God who loved you would allow you to hurt. Right?"

"I guess. But why. . ."

"Has God ever really failed you? Think about it. When your parents died, were you truly left alone? Didn't God provide others to help you?"

"I guess," Kit said again. "That's when Dr. Ellis and I became closer. And Ruth. . .and lots of people from church. . ."

"You see? And as for you being handicapped, you're not the only one, you know. Do you think God doesn't love all those other people that suffer with some sort of physical challenge? You're not the only person He hasn't healed."

"Oh, but I have been healed."

Keith turned his head to stare at her. "How's that?"

"Dad took me to Texas, to some revival meetings. They were wonderful. . .and they prayed for the sick."

"You were prayed for?" The doctor's voice was skeptical.

Kit nodded. "It was unbelievable. Here were all these people looking for help—but the evangelist looked at me and said, 'I've seen you sitting in the aisle day after day—and tonight the Lord has told me to pray especially for you. That's what I'm going to do now.'"

"So you were healed." Kit saw the cynical twist to the doctor's lips.

"Yes. . .and no. Later, it was one more thing that made me wonder if God really loved me. . .but at the time I felt surrounded by so much love. When the man prayed, suddenly all the pain left my body. It was as though a key had unlocked a door inside me, and I was flooded with. . .I don't know. I felt strong and well inside.

"Outside, though, nothing had changed. But from that day on, I began to improve. I didn't need painkillers anymore, not as much. And I got stronger. But still—I felt as though God had let me down. Why would He take the pain but leave me crippled? I've never understood."

She spread her gnarled fingers in her lap. "Someone told me once that God had healed me of the disease, but He didn't restore what the disease had already destroyed. I wanted Him to do it all, though. If He could do part of it, He could do the whole thing, couldn't He? I didn't want to go to doctors anymore. But. . ." She hesitated. "Some people have told me my faith isn't great enough. For a while that made me so angry, I didn't even want to believe in God. But I do believe in Him. I've just had so many doubts. I hate to talk about them; I hate to admit my faith truly isn't as great as it should be."

"And so," Keith said gently, "you've been afraid to confide in anyone. You were afraid they would judge you for your feelings. You were afraid they would let you down too."

Kit's eyes burned. "I don't know why I've told you all this now." She turned her eyes toward the window, blinking away the tears. "Do you think I'm silly?"

"No, I don't. I think you've been through a lot, and your feelings are perfectly understandable. But think now of all God *has* done for you. He gave you a good friend in Dr. Ellis. That man will go to any length to keep you happy and walking. And Ruth—ever since I came to the clinic, I've heard her talk about how wonderful you are. And your parents—even though they're gone now, you were blessed to have them while you were growing up. Not everyone has the security of loving parents." Keith smiled. "I think God *has* shown you how much He loves you in some very special ways."

Kit felt the warmth of his hand on her arm. He touched her without revulsion but with tenderness, and she knew suddenly that Keith's touch only reflected the tenderness that God felt for her too. Her tears spilled over. She felt as though a hard knot inside her, a knot that had been a part of her for years, was finally loosening, falling away, leaving her free. Her face lifted, she closed her eyes, feeling God's love wash over her.

Keith's hand slid down her arm and grasped hers. "Don't ever let people's rejection turn you against God, Kit. Remember, they even rejected Christ when He was here on earth. But people's opinions don't matter, not to God. He loves you. He cares for you." Keith hesitated, and when he spoke again, his voice was clipped. "I care too, Kit."

Kit blinked away her tears. "What?"

Keith's mouth twisted. "You heard me. You wouldn't happen to have a tissue for those tears of yours, would you?"

Kit reached into her purse and pulled out several

tissues. She blew her nose, feeling like a child, but too happy to care. She turned toward Keith. "Would you mind if we prayed?"

"Of course not."

Kit bowed her head. She felt embarrassed, but she needed to confess her fears, not only to God but to Keith as well. "Forgive me, God," she said softly. "Forgive me for not trusting You. Forgive me for not recognizing Your love. I refused to believe You really loved me. I—I was rejecting You, just the way I've felt rejected, wasn't I? I'm sorry. Please help me to trust You now. Thank You for loving me even when I've been afraid to love You . . .or anyone else. Thank You for showing me Your love through Keith, for using his words to open my heart. In Your Son's name, amen."

She opened her eyes, then shut them again as she heard Keith's deep voice say, "Father, thank You for bringing Kit back to a place where she could see how much You do love her. Please be with her during this hard time with her grandmother. Please give her strength. And—and thank You for bringing her into my life. In Christ's name, amen."

Kit lifted her head and smiled shyly at Keith through her tears.

"Feel better?"

She nodded. "I feel free. Thank you, . . .friend." She leaned back and looked out the window, but the smile lingered on her lips. She hadn't felt so unencumbered since before her illness began.

❧

Keith was right; Kit did love his sister's house. Here in the outskirts of the huge metropolis, the wide Mississippi wandered by this peaceful corner, where untouched forests surrounded sloping green lawns.

Keith was right too about his sister's welcome. As soon as Beth saw them, she held out plump welcoming arms. "So this is little Kit. I'm so glad to meet you, dear. I'm eager to know all about you. You know how Keith is—getting information out of him is like prying open a clam."

Beth led them into the living room, still chatting, and any nervousness Kit had felt disappeared. "My husband John is still at work," Beth told her. "Lisa, that's our oldest, is a camp counselor this year. Heidi may be here for lunch, I'm not sure. She's with a friend right now." Beth motioned toward the sofa. "Sit down, sit down. I'll have lunch ready in a few minutes."

"I'd like to show Kit the porch," Keith said. He held his hand out to her, and Kit slipped her fingers into his large warm ones. He led her through sliding glass doors to the redwood deck that overlooked the lawns and river.

Kit leaned against the railing, breathing in the outdoor air. Below her, a small building seemed to float on the water beside the dock.

"Boathouse," Keith said pointing at it. A sleek cruiser was tied beside the dock. "After lunch, I'll take you out for a spin."

Kit's eyes shone, but before she could answer a young girl who looked about thirteen ran through the door, followed by another girl about the same age. "Uncle Keith!"

"Heidi." Keith turned to smile at his niece. "Come here. Meet my friend Kit."

Heidi and her friend looked at Kit with youth's frank curiosity, but their smiles were genuine. "Glad to meet you, Kit," Heidi said. "Uncle Keith's going to take you out in the boat after lunch?"

"Yes, I am," Keith said. "Want to come?"

Heidi flipped her long braids behind her shoulders and

grinned. "Of course. Don't we, Sheila?"

Her friend nodded shyly.

A few minutes later Beth brought plates of food out onto the deck, and they sat down on cushioned redwood chairs beneath the umbrellaed table. Beth had provided an ample lunch of fried chicken, cole slaw, potato salad, homemade bread and jam, and apple pie with ice cream for dessert.

When they were done, Keith leaned back and patted his stomach. "That beat the Colonel's. I'll have to start exercising more or by the time I go home, you'll have me fat as a pig, Beth."

The women and girls laughed at the idea of a fat Keith, but he shook his head sadly. "It's true, it's true." He got to his feet and looked at his sister. "Coming with us, Beth?"

She shook her head. "I have a meeting this afternoon at church. I'll just clean up and leave." She smiled at Kit. "I hope you enjoy yourself this afternoon."

"I already am," Kit answered. "Thank you for the delicious meal."

They helped Beth clear the table, and then Heidi ran to get the keys for the boat. She and her friend scrambled down the path ahead of Keith and Kit.

Keith took Kit's hand and carefully helped her down the curving flagstone path that led to the dock. The ground was smooth, and Kit tried once to let go of his hand, but his fingers gripped hers firmly, as though he were unwilling to release her. As though, Kit thought hesitantly, he were holding her hand because he wanted to, not because she needed help. Joy bubbled inside her; joy and something else that she could not name yet.

The sun caught sparks on the shiny blue and silver boat. Overhead, fluffy clouds drifted in the blue sky. *"God's in*

His Heaven, All's right with the world," thought Kit, quoting a poem she had once heard.

The younger girls already had their life jackets on and were waiting in the boat. They giggled as Keith picked Kit up in his arms and set her carefully in the boat. Surely, Kit thought, it was only her imagination that his hands lingered on her waist as he set her down. He handed her a life jacket, and she turned it around and around, uncertain how to put it on.

Keith grinned and took it from her, then helped her into it and tied it, his fingers quick and efficient. Kit looked down at his hands, her face warm, unable to look up into his face as he stood so close to her.

Keith moved the boat out into the river, and the two girls squealed and giggled as the boat picked up speed. They leaned over the boat's edge, ignoring Keith and Kit. Keith too seemed to be concentrating on the water, his lips set in a frown. No one noticed as Kit began to slide from her seat.

Her hands flayed, trying to find something to grasp, and her feet pushed against the floor, trying to brace herself. Keith turned his head—and then he scooped her into his arms. He set her in front of him, his arms around her as he steered the boat.

For a moment, Kit stood stiffly, embarrassed. Gradually, though, feeling warm and secure, she relaxed. Water sprayed her face, and she laughed.

"Having fun?" Keith's breath tickled her ear.

Laughing as spray chilled her cheeks, Kit nodded. The long ride exhilarated her; that explained why her breath came fast and hard, she told herself, enjoying the warm touch of Keith's arms against her shoulders.

But the vibration of the engine and the rocking of the

boat tired her. She was glad when at last Keith nudged the boat back against the dock.

"Thanks!" the two girls called over their shoulders and ran off up the path.

Keith tied the boat and then lifted Kit out and set her on the ground. She swayed, her legs feeling like rubber, and he laughed and swept her back into his arms, then strode up the hill to the porch. "This disability of yours has some advantages after all," he said softly, looking down at her.

She looked up at him. "What do you mean?"

He laughed again. "Never mind." He set her down on the deck, then took her hand and led her through the sliding doors into the kitchen.

He raided the refrigerator for leftover chicken and salad. "I'm hungry," he said. "What about you?"

Normally, Kit never had much of an appetite, but now her hunger surprised her. "Sounds good. I can't believe I'm hungry again after that lunch."

"Good for you." Keith looked at her solemnly. "I hope you had a good afternoon, Kit. I wish you could stay longer. Unfortunately, I have a dinner meeting I can't miss."

Kit colored. "Please. Don't apologize. I've had a wonderful afternoon. I can't thank you. . .can't tell you how much. . ." Her voice trailed away, unable to find the words to express her feelings.

Keith squeezed her hand and pulled her closer. "I'm glad." He hesitated. "Did you—did you hear the girls talking about Valley Fair? I'm taking them to it sometime in the next day or two." He looked quickly down into Kit's face. "Want to come along?"

"You don't have to, Keith. I don't want to be a nuisance."

"Don't be silly. I want you to come. Heidi and her friend will desert me as soon as we get inside the amusement park, and I'll be left wandering aimlessly with a container of cotton candy in my hand. You'd be doing me a favor if you'd come with me." He smiled. "Really."

"Well. . .you're sure you wouldn't rather ask someone else? I know you probably promised Dr. Ellis you would look out for me, but I'm fine now, really."

"I don't want anyone else," Keith said firmly. "If you won't go, I'll be alone. You wouldn't want that, would you?" He kept his voice light, but he admitted to himself that he really meant his words. He did want Kit with him . . .and no one else would do. After this afternoon, he was eager to see her again, to watch the light that filled her face when something pleased her.

"All right then." Kit smiled.

She was still smiling as Keith left her in her grandmother's hallway.

Meanwhile, Keith drove to his conference, his mind filled with the memory of Kit's soft warmth in his arms. For a moment, he thought of his list of standards for a woman. He shook his head. His ideal woman seemed not nearly as interesting now, certainly not as interesting as the image of Kit's spray-washed face and wide blue eyes.

eight

But as for me, this secret is not revealed to me. . .
Daniel 2:30a

🙠

Kit heard the click-click of Augusta's heels on the kitchen linoleum and turned toward her aunt with a smile. "How was work?"

Augusta poured herself a cup of coffee and sank into a kitchen chair. She took a long, slow swallow. "Work was fine. Exhausting. The bus was late." She twisted to look at the clock. "I hope you haven't had to hold up dinner." She sipped her coffee. "What did you do today, Katalina?"

"I went out for a while."

Augusta sat down her coffee cup. "Kit. Surely you know how dangerous it is for a young woman to wander alone on the streets. Particularly, considering your. . . This isn't a small town like you're used to."

Kit smiled. "I wasn't alone, Aunt Augusta. A friend of mine picked me up. We had lunch at his sister's in Anoka."

"This was someone you know?" Augusta looked at her niece doubtfully. "Not some stranger you picked up. . .?"

"Of course not. I was with Dr. Long, the one who came with me to Minneapolis. His sister lives here, in Anoka, I mean. Dr. Long has a conference in Minneapolis this week. My orthopedist, Dr. Ellis, sort of put me in his charge, I suppose." She grimaced.

"Well, I suppose that's all right then." Augusta's long fingers turned her coffee cup round and round. "Then

again, one never knows who one can trust these days."
She stood up and put her cup in the sink. "I'll go change
for dinner."

Kit followed her to the bedroom to drop the book she
had been reading on her bed. Her aunt glanced at the lurid
cover, a picture of a dead man laid out on the floor. She
shuddered. "I wouldn't think that does much to improve
your mind, Kit. I have some good books you might better
be reading—Billy Graham, Charles Swindoll, Dobson. . ."

"I know, Aunt Augusta. I read those too. But sometimes I just like a good mystery."

Her aunt glanced at the cover again, and Kit saw that
she was genuinely repulsed by the picture. "Please. . ."
her aunt said, "at least turn it over or something. I'd rather
not have to look at it."

Kit looked at her aunt's pale face, and she realized the
picture must remind Augusta of her father's death.
Quickly, Kit tucked the book out of sight. "I'm sorry. I'll
keep it out of your way."

Augusta turned quickly away, bumping into the stack
of photo albums Sally must have placed on the dresser.
Gingerly, she picked one up. "I haven't seen these for
years." She flipped it open, then snapped it shut. "Not
now. If you will leave, Kit, I'll dress. We can look at these
later."

She brought the albums with her when she came to the
table several minutes later. Lars looked up from his seat
at the table and reached for one of the albums. "What's
this?"

Kit watched as her aunt, looking almost fearful, opened
another one.

"Hey, look at this," Lars said, pointing to a photograph.
"Is that my old man? Look at the fancy mustache."

Augusta leaned over to look. "Yes, yes, that's Uncle Edmund." She closed the album she held. "Who brought these down anyway?"

"I did," Kit said. "Gramma asked me to."

Augusta turned to stare at her. "Surely Mother knew better than to send you, of all people. . ." She shook her head, and then added firmly, "I'll take them right back up to where they belong. Mother must be more confused than I thought."

"I think she knew I could do it," Kit defended her grandmother. "The steps were solid and I was careful."

Her aunt glanced at her. "Oh. Yes, of course," she said absently, and Kit realized she had been worried about something besides Kit's disability. "Nevertheless. . ." Augusta set the album on the sideboard. "I'll see these get back where they belong. Don't you bother with them, Kit. I don't see why Mother wanted to drag the old things down anyway."

"She wanted to see pictures of Claus," Kit said. "It made her happy."

"Mother." Augusta leaped to her feet. "I haven't even been in to see her since I got home. How is she? And where is Sally? Is something wrong? Oh, what was the matter with me, not even thinking to. . . Oh, dear. . ."

She turned to leave, but Kit put her hand on her aunt's arm. "Gramma's fine, Aunt Augusta. And when you were late, I helped Sally get dinner ready. She should have it on the table any minute now. She's just checking on Gramma first. Don't worry."

Her aunt sank back into her chair as Sally bustled into the room. "Augusta. Good, you're home."

"And Mother?"

"No change. Don't fret yourself, Augusta."

Sally got the food quickly on the table, and she kept up a stream of cheerful conversation. The dinner was more pleasant than the one the night before, but Kit couldn't help but compare it to the light and happy conversation around Beth's picnic table. Lars and Edmund carried an atmosphere of darkness and bitterness with them, and Kit was relieved when at last the meal was over.

Lars and Edmund shuffled back to the living room, and Kit helped Sally clear the table. Augusta picked up the albums and headed toward the stairs, her lips pressed tightly together. Kit watched her go, sorry not to have had more time to examine the albums, and then followed Sally into the kitchen.

Kit had just picked up a dishtowel and reached for a plate, when a scream rent the air. It was followed by a tumbling thump-thumpety-thump. Kit turned to exchange a stunned glance with Sally, then threw down her towel and limped quickly toward the stairs. "Aunt Augusta!" she called.

She found her aunt lying at the bottom of the stairs. Her left foot stuck out beneath her at a strange angle. Sally knelt beside her and gently probed the ankle. "Hurts?"

Augusta winced and nodded.

"I don't think it's broken, though. Here," Sally put a large arm around Augusta's thin shoulders, "let me help you up. You just lean on me."

Frustrated that she could not help, Kit watched Sally help her aunt into the bedroom. This was one of those times when she most hated her handicap. Tears of self-pity welled in her eyes, and her mind turned toward God with automatic accusations. Then she stopped. She remembered her conversation with Keith.

Jesus loved her. He loved her enough to die for her, to

provide her with people who loved her. Like Job, she had lost her family and her health, but like Job she would try to keep her faith strong. In the end, Job had been rewarded for trusting God, and his calamities had been far worse than her own. No, this time she would not wallow in her feelings of self-pity as she had so many times before; this time she would turn to her Father for help. She felt peace flow through her heart.

She opened the door to the stairway and saw the albums scattered across the steps. Half lying on the stairs, straining her arms out straight, she managed to grab them all. She stacked them in her arms, then decided to check on her grandmother. Clara must have heard Augusta's scream, and Sally was too busy with Augusta right now to go to her.

She stuck her head in Clara's door. The old woman's head was back against the pillow, her eyes closed, her face relaxed. Her sleep must have been so deep that even the scream failed to rouse her. Kit tiptoed across the floor and put the albums on a dresser. For a moment, she hesitated, looking at her grandmother's face. Was such a deep sleep normal?

Kit shrugged. After all, her grandmother was old and ill. Sally had said she would sleep more and more these days, and obviously she was right. Kit turned and limped across the hall to her aunt's room.

Augusta lay on her bed, her leg on two pillows, a cold pack on her ankle. Kit looked at Sally. "How is it?"

"She'll be fine, dearie. I'm pretty sure it's just a sprain."

"She'll need x-rays, won't she?"

"X-rays!" Augusta's voice was horrified.

Sally patted her arm. "Now, Augusta, don't work yourself up. Kit was only making a suggestion." Sally narrowed her eyes at Kit. "Weren't you, dearie? But I really don't think x-rays are necessary."

"I just thought—" Kit started, but Sally interrupted her.

"Like I said, Augusta, it's only a sprain. Course if you'd feel better, we can take you to the hospital for x-rays."

Augusta fell back against the bed. "No. If you say it's only a sprain—" She turned to Kit. "Sally is always right about these things."

Kit bit her lip, longing to argue. She sighed. "How do you feel, Aunt Augusta?"

Augusta shook her head, her face white. "I just don't understand it. I've been up and down those steps a thousand times. How could I have fallen like that?"

Sally adjusted the cold compress on Augusta's ankle. "There, now, don't fret yourself. Accidents will happen. Maybe an x-ray would put your mind to rest."

Augusta shook her head. "I can't. I have to go to work in the morning. You said it was only sprained, so there's no need. . . I must go to work. . ." Panic flashed in her eyes.

"One day of sick leave surely won't hurt anything," Kit protested.

"No, no, no. I haven't missed a day for sick leave in twenty years. I mustn't miss work."

"Well," said Kit, "you certainly have sick time coming to you."

Augusta turned her head back and forth against the pillow. "No. When Mother. . .goes, then I'll take it, I'll need it. . .but not now. Please. . ."

Sally pressed her lips tightly together. Hands on her wide hips, she stared down at Augusta. "I think you better get those x-rays after all. I'll not be having anyone saying I didn't do my best for you." She glanced at Kit. "Now,

I'll get you some pills for the pain, and those other pills to help you sleep. Tonight you *will* take them." She turned to Kit once more. "Kit, please see that she takes them."

Kit hesitated. "I'll remind her."

Sally's forehead creased. "Maybe I should stay over."

"No, no, not on my account," Augusta protested. "Besides, I have no bed to offer you."

"Well," Sally looked from Augusta to Kit, "all right. But you must promise to call me if you need me, even if it's the middle of the night. Kit, you can look in on Clara. If either she or Augusta needs me, I can be here in less than half an hour."

Augusta smiled faintly. "Thank you, Sally. You've always been a good friend."

Kit left the two older women alone and went into the living room. Edmund stared at her, his pale eyes glittering. "What happened?"

"Aunt Augusta fell."

Lars snorted. "Old lady should be more careful on the stairs."

Kit looked at him thoughtfully. "I don't think I mentioned that she fell on the stairs. How did you know?"

Lars shrugged. "A deaf man could have told you, from the racket she made coming down."

Kit shook her head in disgust. "Then why didn't you come to help her?"

Lars shrugged once again. "That's what Sally's paid for. Old lady should know better than to climb those dangerous stairs."

"I was on those stairs this morning. The stairs are steep, yes, but not otherwise dangerous."

"Well, good for you. Just goes to show the old girl's even more tottery than I thought."

Kit let out her breath in exasperation. Without bothering to say anything further to Edmund or Lars, she went back to the bedroom.

"Is Sally with Gramma?" she asked her aunt.

Her aunt nodded weakly. "Yes, she's getting her ready for the night."

Kit sat on the edge of Augusta's bed. "Feeling any better?"

Augusta waved her hands. "I'm fine. It's just. . .it's just so strange." She looked up into her niece's face and frowned. "Katalina, I'm almost sure the reason I fell is that a step gave way beneath me. Sally said she didn't notice anything like that when she helped me up—but. . . Did you see anything, Kit?"

Kit shook her head. "I just picked up the albums, and I didn't see anything. I can check again."

Her aunt's frown deepened. "Kit, if there are loose steps, promise me you won't try to go up there again."

"When I went up this morning, I know each step was solid, Aunt Augusta. Believe me, I checked each one."

Her aunt shook her head. "It doesn't make any sense. I did not slip. At least," her voice wavered, "I don't think I did. I was so sure it was the step. . .but if you say. . ."

"Wait." Kit stood up. "Let me check." She went to the stairway and swung open the narrow door. In the dim light, she could see nothing unusual, but she climbed up the first three steps so she could see the top of the stairway better.

Her stomach twisted. Almost at the top, a step board hung loose, swinging from a single nail. Kit swallowed. Augusta's fall had not been an accident.

She was overwhelmed with a longing to call Keith. She couldn't bother him, though; she didn't even know where he would be tonight. She leaned against the door frame, her fingers gripping the wood until her knuckles turned white.

"Oh, Lord," she whispered, "what is going on?"

nine

He that. . .layeth up deceit within him;
When he speaketh fair, believe him not.
Proverbs 26:24-25a

෨

Someone had tampered with the step in a deliberate attempt to injure or scare someone. Was the sabotage meant for her—or for her aunt? Why? Who wanted to harm either of them? Aunt Augusta was surely harmless enough . . . As for herself—Kit was forced to smile at the idea that anyone would see her as a threat.

Her smile quickly faded, though, and she shuddered. If she had been the one to carry those albums up the stairs, she could easily have been killed. Her aunt's fall had been bad enough, but Kit would not have been able to break her fall at all. She groaned out loud and her heart pounded. She longed to call Keith.

She gulped, swallowing down her fear. With her eyes closed, she envisioned Keith's calm, skeptical face. Mentally, she explained to him her suspicions—and saw him shake his head. "Have you any proof?" she imagined him asking, his voice cynical.

"Not really," she whispered, "but. . ."

"You're sure your fears aren't a result of your overactive imagination? After all, at this very moment you're in the midst of an imaginary conversation."

Kit sighed ruefully. No, she had nothing but conjecture. As much as she longed to, she could not run to the doctor with her vague suspicions.

After all, she had only known the doctor for a few days. Thinking of him so often, relying on him so heavily, was probably unhealthy. "God," she whispered, "help me to rely on You. What should I do? Who can I talk to?"

Gramma? Definitely not. Augusta, then? No, she would only become even more upset than she already was. Certainly not either Lars or Uncle Edmund. She could imagine the scorn in Lars' voice. In fact, she realized that Lars was the person she could most easily picture trying to hurt someone. But why would he? What reason could he have?

Who else could she talk to, though? Sally? Why not? At that moment Sally herself stepped out of Gramma Clara's bedroom, closing the door behind her. Kit smiled and breathed a sigh of relief.

"Sally, come here. I want to show you something." She waited until Sally was beside her at the foot of the stairs, and then Kit pointed upward at the broken step. "Look at that. That step was solid this morning when I went up to the second floor. I know it was."

Sally stood with her hands on her hips looking up at the stairs. "My, dearie, that does look wicked. No wonder Augusta fell." She shook her head. "Someone should have checked those stairs before. That step has probably been loosening up for some time. It was just an accident waiting to happen."

"No," Kit said. "I told you. All those steps were perfectly solid when I went up them this morning. I tested each one."

Sally's eyes narrowed as she looked at Kit's face. "More likely, dearie, you just had a lucky escape. How could the step have been solid this morning, when by the time

Augusta stepped on it, it obviously wasn't? You're not making any sense, dearie."

Kit bit her lip. She knew arguing would only be a waste of her time. The facts seemed so obvious to her, but apparently they didn't to Sally. Kit couldn't very well accuse any one, and so she said nothing. Helplessly, she looked from the broken step to Sally's good-natured face.

Sally patted Kit's shoulder. "This has been a shock for you, dearie, hasn't it? Your aunt getting hurt like this on top of everything else. You've had nothing but problems ever since you came, poor dear. As though your grandmother being so sick wasn't enough for you to cope with, first you had to contend with those two ghouls, Edmund and Lars, then Augusta's nightmares, now this frightful accident." Her eyes rested thoughtfully on Kit's pale face. "You do know that's all this was, don't you—an accident? You're not letting your imagination run away with you now, are you, dearie?"

Kit shrugged and turned toward her room. "Thanks, Sally. I guess I just wanted to talk to someone."

Sally's broad face creased into a smile. "I'm always ready to listen, dearie. But it's late now, and if you're all right. . .?" Kit nodded. "Well, then I best be getting on home. Make sure Augusta takes those pills now, you hear?"

Kit nodded again, though she couldn't meet Sally's eyes.

"Well, goodbye then, dearie. I'll be seeing you tomorrow."

❧

Early the next morning, much earlier than her usual time, Sally returned. "I've already called the doctor, Augusta," she said, "so you can just forget about going to work. You have an appointment to have that ankle checked."

Augusta's pale face grew whiter, but she allowed Sally

to push her toward the door. Kit watched from the kitchen table, a coffee cup in her hand, glad that Augusta would have her ankle properly examined. While Augusta and Sally were gone, she would have a chance to spend more time with Gramma Clara.

As she went out the back door, however, Sally looked back over her shoulder at Kit. "Clara is very tired this morning," she said. "Please don't disturb her, dearie."

Reluctantly, Kit nodded.

She stood up and put her teacup in the sink. The morning air was already hot and muggy, pressing against her skin even as loneliness threatened to smother her. She hesitated in the kitchen doorway, but she knew she would never be able to endure the dark living room; with a sigh, she went back to her bedroom and picked up her book.

After a few moments, she slapped it shut. "Lord, why am I here anyway? No one but Gramma really wants me here, and I've scarcely had a chance to see her. What am I to do about that broken step? And what about my missing jewelry box?"

She heard the front door open and went into the living room in time to see Lars amble into the room. He flung himself down on the couch with a grunt. "When will breakfast be ready?"

"You'll have to get it yourself." Kit's lips were tight, and she felt no guilt for her rudeness. "Sally has taken Aunt Augusta to the doctor."

Edmund shuffled in and took his seat in the corner. He held out a trembling hand toward Kit and whined, "Come talk to an old man, Katalina."

Kit hesitated, then pulled out the piano bench and perched on its edge, wishing she had never left her bedroom. Uncle Edmund's glittering eyes rested on her face, and then he smiled.

Something about that smile sent a flood of memories washing over Kit, memories of pain and humiliation she had tried to forget. She shuddered, trying to push the past away, but behind Uncle Edmund's face she saw again the cruelty in the face of the drunk hospital porter who had smashed her helpless body against the wall; she saw the cold eyes of some of the nurses as they administered experimental medicine to her, not caring how ill it made her feel; and she heard again the careless laughter of the hospital attendants as they ignored the patients' calls.

Kit shook her head. She took a deep breath and firmly closed the door against the memories. God loved her. He had rescued her, had brought her to Dr. Ellis' clinic. The first time she had entered the clinic's doors, she had felt the staff's compassion, had sensed the presence of Christ's love. And now Keith had helped her to open her heart to that love. No, she would not permit herself to be washed under by the past.

A shadow still clung to her heart, though. She looked away from her uncle's face. "Help me, Lord," she said under her breath. "Please help me." Instantly, she saw in her mind's eyes Keith's broad shoulders, the twist of his cynical mouth; she smiled faintly. Why should that mental image bring her such comfort?

She shrugged, and then she straightened her shoulders. Uncle Edmund was a pathetic old man. She would not give him the power to hurt her. Deliberately, she smiled at the old man. "What are you thinking about, Uncle Edmund?"

Edmund looked down at the hourglass in his hands, and then he shrugged. "Look at the sand. I wonder if it understands what it's doing, do you think? Does it know it has a purpose—or does it just mindlessly slide from one end of the glass to the other?" His pale eyes watched the white stream of sand, but his face had a slack, unfocused look. He sighed. "At least the sand does have a purpose, whether it knows it or not. Not like me. For me. . .," he sighed and clutched the hourglass tighter against his sunken chest, "for me things just get more vague. . ."

Kit watched him for a moment, not knowing what to say. "What *is* your purpose in life?" she asked at last. "Surely you must have one."

The old man's thin shoulders lifted and fell, and then he glanced at Kit with a hint of craftiness. "Happiness . . .wealth. . .like everybody else. What else is there?"

"Those aren't my goals," Kit said softly. "I'm more interested in the things that will last for eternity."

Edmund stared at Kit's face, but as she watched, she saw his eyes glaze over, and his expression become bewildered. "I will get what I want. . .one day. Not yet . . .but I will have it. . .I will have it all. . ." Behind his clouded expression, she saw a strange intensity that made her shiver.

"What is it you want, Uncle?"

Edmund turned over the hourglass and watched the sand for a long moment. When at last he spoke, his voice seemed to come from far away. "They kept me from what I desire, you know. Wasn't my fault. They did it. Nothing I could do."

"What are you talking about, Uncle Edmund?"

"Clara, Clara and. . .Kat. Kat went off and left me, went off, and then Clara. Left me stranded. She didn't care about me." His voice was a whine once more.

"Couldn't you have followed them to America sooner?

You weren't helpless surely."

Edmund's head jerked, but his glittering gaze remained fixed on the hourglass, still clasped tightly between his blue-veined hands.

Kit shuddered again, though she wasn't sure exactly why. She forced herself to smile. "Gramma says you were quite the ladies' man when you were younger."

The old man grunted. "Didn't matter to Kat. She left me anyway. She wouldn't listen. Never would. We could have had a good life. *Ya*, we could have."

"I guess," Kit said softly, "Katalina just didn't love you as much as you loved her. That must have been very sad for you." Privately, Kit thanked God this pathetic old man was not her grandfather.

Edmund leaned back in his chair and closed his eyes. The veins on his neck bulged blue against the chalky white of his skin. After a moment, his eyes shot open and he stared with revulsion at his son.

Kit also turned her head and saw that Lars was snoring on the sofa, his thick arms slack across his chest. She heard Edmund sigh, and when she looked back at him, the look he gave her was filled with something that looked very like malice. Then he closed his eyes once again.

With a chill creeping down her spine, Kit struggled to get to her feet, but her uncle's voice stopped her. "Kat loved me, you know. She did. Always the butterfly. So pretty, so bright. And her smile. Why, it's for me!" His faded eyes opened and they stared into space, as though they saw something invisible to Kit. "It is for me. It is!" He shook his head. "Uncle Al again. Always in the way."

"Wasn't Katalina his niece?"

Edmund frowned, then turned his eyes toward Kit. "Kat, you can't spend all your life with your uncle. You have your own life to live. You belong to me. Let's go away now, today. Leave the old man. You'll do better on your own without him. You don't need him."

"Do better?" Kit asked, unwilling to break the strange spell that gripped her uncle. Maybe if she went along with him, she would learn more about her grandmother.

Her uncle nodded. "That's right. Kat. She played until you wanted to laugh, to weep. She wrote songs too." His voice grew rough. "But it was always that old man who came first with her. His needs. His career. His career!" Edmund sniffed. "He was a hymn writer, that's all. Why should Kat waste herself doting on an old man like that? I tried. I tried to talk to her, to make her see what she was doing, but she wouldn't listen. She wouldn't leave that doting old fool." Edmund grunted, a strange noise from deep in his throat. "So I helped."

He laughed, his voice still strangely deep. "I dressed the old man. I put him to bed. He was as good as dead, yet she wouldn't leave him. Said he was her uncle. Said he needed her. She loved him, she said. Nonsense." He lowered his voice, and his face turned toward Kit, but she knew he no longer saw her.

"She would have come away with me. . .in time. The fire, I thought that would make her come. Not my fault, though. I didn't know the tree was so dry. I only lit the candles to please her." He paused and moistened his lips with his tongue. "She screamed and then she beat at the fire. She tried to save that old man. Worthless old man. I held her back, wouldn't let her risk herself. I saved her. I saved her." He shook his head back and forth, back and forth. "No, you can't go back, Kat. Let him go. He only screamed the once. Better this way. . . Kat, don't leave me. Kat, I love you. . ."

His eyes focused on Kit's face once again. "You left me," he accused. "You left me for your farmer. I hate your farmer. Your fault, you know. All your fault. . .and Clara's too. You shouldn't have come back, Kat. *Ya*, you were better off dead. Like always, you make trouble . . .make me remember. . ."

Kit shivered as he sagged back in his chair. He looked down at the hourglass, then once again turned it over. Kit pushed herself to her feet. She limped out of the living room as fast as she could, feeling as though the fingers of Edmund's hate were reaching after her, trying to grasp her in their monstrous hold.

She shut her bedroom door firmly. "Lord," she said out loud, "it's not my imagination that there is something very wrong in this place. I don't think it's Lars after all. I think it's Uncle Edmund." She paced across the bedroom floor, then back again. "He thinks I'm Katalina. Oh, Lord, what do I do? I'm frightened. I can't stand this hate, this fear. . ."

She rubbed her forehead. Although she seldom suffered headaches, now her temples throbbed. She sank on her bed and closed her eyes, trying to ease the pain. Why, she asked herself, should she be afraid of that old man? He was only a pathetic shell.

At least she had learned something, something important. She knew now why her grandmother had run away. Because of his selfish jealousy, Edmund had let a helpless old man burn to death.

Thoughtfully, Kit twisted the gold bracelet on her arm. Everyone had run away from Edmund: Katalina, Clara, even his wife. All he had left to show for his misspent life was Lars—and his hate. Almost, Kit felt sorry for her uncle.

His words had made clear that he hated everyone, even Gramma Clara. But why? Why should he hate his own sister? He had followed her to America and they had been reunited. Gramma Clara obviously cared about him. He had no reason to hate her, not that Kit could see. She shook her head. Something didn't fit, pieces of the puzzle were still missing. Unless, she thought, his feelings were totally irrational, with no basis in reality whatsoever. And that would mean—Kit shivered—that he was insane.

She sensed that her coming here had opened doors long locked shut. She was the catalyst, stirring to life some ancient, dormant thing, starting a dangerous course of events she did not comprehend, for all that she had set them into motion.

She shook her head. Secrets. Too many secrets. She lifted her chin, determined to uncover the secrets, to bring them out into the light of day, not only for her own peace of mind but for the safety of her aunt. Her relatives needed to let their secrets be uncovered, for the secrets were unbalancing their minds, turning this home into a house haunted by the past.

If only Keith were here. Surely, his calm logic would be able to make sense out of this mystery. Kit sighed and once again put the doctor's image out of her mind. After all, maybe logic would do no good in the face of the fierce, irrational emotions that filled this house.

Kit picked up her book again, but she was relieved when she heard someone at the back door. She hurried to the kitchen.

"Please, dearie," called Sally, "could you hold the door open for us? A little wider. That's good."

Augusta hobbled in on crutches, her ankle firmly bandaged. She slumped into a kitchen chair, rubbing her armpits. "Kit," she gasped, "how did a little thing like you ever manage to get around on crutches?"

"You get used to them. After a little while you won't be so sore."

"I don't know." Nervously, Augusta ran her hand up and down one crutch.

Sally left them to check on Clara, but was soon back. "Clara is just fine, Augusta. Sound asleep, just like I left her. You didn't need to worry." She patted Augusta's shoulder. "It's you who needs the nurse now."

Augusta frowned. "I don't know what to do. There's so much that needs to be done. How can I do everything with a sprained ankle?"

"It is just a sprain?" Kit asked.

Augusta nodded. "*Ya*. You're right, it's only a sprain, I should get up and get lunch ready."

"Pooh." Sally's large hand pushed Augusta back into her seat. "You just relax. I'll just fix sandwiches and a salad. You're usually at work now, you know, and I'd be fixing lunch anyway. So calm down."

Augusta's thin lips pressed together. "But since I'm here, I should help. . ."

"No," Kit said. "Sally's right. Just rest for once."

Her aunt once again struggled to get to her feet. "I think I could manage to dust. I'll do that. . ."

"No, you won't." Sally once more pushed Augusta firmly back into her chair. "You'll stay right there. I'll see to whatever needs doing."

Kit looked at Sally thoughtfully, noticing how easily she commanded Aunt Augusta. Perhaps that explained their long friendship; Aunt Augusta needed to lean on someone strong like Sally.

Kit helped Sally get the lunch on the table. When she

went into the living room to call the two men, she found them both in unusually good humor. To her surprise, she could see nothing of the hateful old man who had talked to her earlier; in fact, Edmund looked more alert than she had ever seen him, and he even smiled when she told him that lunch was ready. Lars too was more polite and pleasant than she had seen him before.

As a result, lunch was not as tense as some of the other meals she had eaten in this house. When they had finished eating, however, Lars once again lit up his cigar, and Aunt Augusta's lips pressed anxiously together. Kit could not help but wish she could leave this house. How much better had been the love she had sensed in Keith's sister's house. How long had Gramma Clara put up with this. . .or had things been different when she was up and around?

Kit went back to her bedroom, feeling restless. The house had a tense, waiting feeling that grated on her nerves, made her edgy. As she opened her door, however, the feeling grew only stronger. Her eyes fell on her suitcase, sticking out oddly from behind the door.

She gulped. Someone had moved her case. Her hands shaking, she hauled the suitcase onto the bed and opened it. Her mouth dropped open.

There, nestled snugly in the bottom of the case just as she had last seen it, was her jewelry box. Gingerly, she reached and opened it. The few pieces of jewelry she kept inside were still there; she was not really surprised, since the pieces were not valuable. She ran her fingers along the box's polished surface, but she found not a scratch to mar its smoothness.

She clutched the box against her and frowned. She was relieved to have the box back—but who had taken it in the first place? Had the same person returned it? And why? One more puzzle piece that didn't fit. Somehow, though, she knew this little box played a part in the frightening drama that was unfolding.

She heard the clump, clump of Augusta's crutches and hastily returned the box to the suitcase. By the time her aunt entered the room, Kit was on the bed reading her Bible.

🙟

Keith Long shifted his long legs. His face, however, he kept still, revealing no hint of the restlessness that gripped him. His attention wandered from the conference speaker, and once again, as it had so many times during the past day, Kit's image filled his mind. His lips quirked, remembering her face, her laughter, the feel of her in his arms. He wished he could call her, but he could hardly just get up and leave the conference.

His smile faded, and he was gripped with the certainty that Kit needed him. He shook his head at himself; never before had he been given to such fancies. Still, he reminded himself, prayer never hurt. Mentally, his eyes still fixed on the speaker with every semblance of attention, he lifted Kit before the God they both served.

ten

They encourage themselves in an evil matter:
they commune of laying snares privily;
they say, Who shall see them? Psalm 64:5

❧

With a sigh of relief, Augusta sank onto her bed, leaning her crutches against the wall beside her.

"Anything I can do for you?" asked Kit.

Her aunt shook her head. "*Nej tack*, Kit. No, thank you."

"Would you like me to leave so you can rest?"

"No. I. . .I don't feel much like sleeping." Her eyes begged Kit to stay.

Kit closed her Bible and set it on the night stand. She would have liked to ask her aunt about the jewelry box—but she had promised Gramma Clara not to discuss it with anyone. Maybe, though, she could approach the subject another way.

"Have you noticed anything missing around here?" she asked, her voice offhand.

Augusta turned her head toward Kit. "Why. . .I haven't missed anything. Have you?"

Kit noticed that her aunt did not meet her eyes. She studied the older woman's pale face thoughtfully. "You didn't by any chance empty out my suitcase, did you, Aunt Augusta? To help me unpack, I mean." Although she chose her words carefully, even to her own ears, her question sounded like an accusation.

Her aunt flushed. "Why would I want to go through

your suitcase, Kit? What are you suggesting?"

Kit sighed. "I'm sorry, Aunt Augusta. It's nothing. I just—I just mislaid something. I was hoping you had seen it. But it's not important."

Augusta visibly relaxed. She reached down and pulled off her shoes, then lay back on the bed with a sigh. She gave Kit a weak smile. "I guess I am tired after all." Closing her eyes, she turned her face away from Kit, and a few minutes later, her breathing slowed, became deep and rhythmic. Kit waited a moment longer to be sure her aunt was truly asleep, and then she pushed herself to her feet and tiptoed across the room.

She walked slowly down the hall to the dining room. Though the house was larger than her own apartment back in Kearney, still the small rooms made her feel cramped and uneasy. She missed the sense of openness in her own apartment, the informality and friendliness. She missed Ruth and her other friends. She missed. . .

She took a deep breath and faced her thoughts squarely. Despite the fact she had known him for such a short time, the person she was truly missing the most was Dr. Keith Long. If only she could call him.

She glanced at her watch. He would be at his convention now. She could hardly disturb him there. She found her handbag, though, and checked to make sure she still had the card he had given her with his phone number on it. With the card clutched in her hand, she took a deep breath, willing herself to relax.

She glanced down at the numbers he had written in his firm, dark hand, and she realized they were his sister's phone number—so she couldn't call him now anyway. But maybe later. . .

Just thinking about hearing his voice made her feel

better. She picked up a magazine from the sideboard and sat down to read it. Leafing through the pages, she had just found an interesting-looking article when she heard a moan from Augusta's bedroom.

She threw down the magazine and rushed to her aunt's bed. Augusta lay curled up like a child, her hair across her face, her hands pressed tight against her eyes.

"Aunt Augusta, what's wrong? What is it?"

"Oh, oh. . .I don't know." After a moment, her aunt took her hands away from her eyes and stared up at Kit. "Another nightmare. A horrible one." She reached out a trembling hand and clutched Kit's arm. "What am I to do? I'm scared."

Kit sat next to her on the edge of the bed. "Why are you scared, Aunt Augusta? It was just a dream."

Her aunt shook her head. "My nightmares. . .they're back again. Just like before." Once again she covered her face with her hands. "I'm so afraid. . .afraid of losing my mind. Oh, why are they coming back again? What am I going to do?"

Despite herself, Kit felt her aunt's terror ripple along her own skin. She gripped her aunt's hand, trying to calm her. "Tell me about your nightmare, Aunt Augusta," she said gently, forcing her own fear away. "Maybe that will help. Then we can fight it together."

"I can't." Her aunt moaned. "I can't. It was too awful. I don't want to think about it." She shuddered, then stared at Kit, her eyes wild. "I mustn't think about it. They told me not to think about it."

"What's going on?" asked Sally's voice from the doorway. She marched into the room, her cheerful face growing sober as she took in Augusta's distress. "What's wrong, Augusta?"

Kit answered for her aunt. "Another nightmare. I was just suggesting that talking about it might help."

"Oh, no." Augusta's trembling fingers picked at the bed cover. "It was too awful."

Sally joined Kit on the edge of Augusta's bed. "Why not, Augusta?" the nurse coaxed. "Tell us. It might help you feel better." Her weight tilted the bed toward the floor, and Kit had to brace her feet to keep from sliding off. "Everyone has nightmares," Sally continued. "Tell us about it, Augusta." Kit heard the note of command in her voice.

Apparently, Augusta heard it too. She closed her eyes and swallowed hard, then said obediently, "I was at home with Mother and Father. They were both there—and the strange thing was, Uncle Edmund was there too." Her voice shook and she looked from Sally to Kit. "That can't be, though, can it?"

"It was only a dream," Kit soothed. "Anything can happen in a dream."

"Yes." Augusta took a deep breath. "That's true, isn't it?"

"What happened?" Sally prompted.

"Well," Augusta hesitated, "Uncle Edmund came in the room, all smiles. He and Father played some kind of game. As they played, their voices got louder and louder and louder." Augusta covered her ears as though she could still hear the noise of their voices. "Uncle Edmund jumped up then—and at the same time, Father sank down. Uncle Edmund ran away. I screamed at him, screamed for him to come back, but he pushed me down. I fell down beside Father. . .fell so hard that I broke into little pieces." She shuddered. "And then I woke up."

Sally looked at Augusta through narrowed eyes. "Does

this mean anything to you?"

Augusta shook her head. "I. . .I don't know. I. . .I don't understand." Her voice sounded like a bewildered child's, Kit thought.

"It was just a nightmare," Kit said firmly. "It doesn't have to make any sense. It's over now. Right, Sally?"

She looked at the nurse, waiting for her support, but Sally only reached for one of the medicine bottles beside the bed, her broad face puckered with anxiety. "Kit, please get me some water."

Together, Sally and Kit got Augusta comfortable once again. They left her lying back against her pillow, drowsy from the pill Sally had given her. Kit followed Sally back into the kitchen. Together, they sat down at the table for a cup of tea.

"You don't believe Aunt Augusta's dream was so innocent, do you, Sally?"

Sally leaned back in her seat, making the chair creak. She shook her head. "Her nightmares concern me, dearie, and that's the truth." She paused, as though searching for words. "Claus died of a heart condition," she said at last. "He died because Augusta didn't bring him his pills quick enough. All these years, Augusta has blamed herself. . .as she would, naturally, since she truly was to blame. And at the time, she literally 'went to pieces.'"

Kit leaned forward. "Like in her dreams."

Sally nodded. "That's right. Her subconscious has never gotten over her father's death, has never been able to deal with her own guilt."

Kit considered Sally's words. She realized there was a subtle difference in the nurse's version of the story, a different emphasis that didn't quite match what Gramma Clara had told her. "Gramma was there," she said. "Right there, I mean."

Sally nodded again. "She was there. But she wouldn't ever talk about it afterward. I've always supposed she wanted to protect her daughter, make Augusta's part in her father's death seem as small as possible." Sally shook her head, her plump face sad. "I hate to say it, but Augusta has never been too stable since then. I'm afraid . . .I'm afraid that all she would need is some big upset, and. . ." The nurse shrugged her shoulders and held her palms up. "She'd fall into little pieces again."

Kit looked down into her teacup. "So that's the reason for the taboo on speaking of the incident? Because of how Aunt Augusta might react?"

Sally sipped her tea, then looked at Kit over the cup's rim. "Makes sense, doesn't it?"

Kit frowned. "But," she said slowly, "if Aunt Augusta caused her father's death, and that's what's bothering her— then why was Uncle Edmund in her dream?"

Sally's pudgy hands gripped the fragile cup. "I don't know, dearie. That bothers me as well. But who can explain a person's subconscious? I'm no psychologist."

"*Could* Uncle Edmund have been there when her father died?"

"Hardly." Sally smiled, but Kit noticed her wide mouth was tight. "You forget, Edmund came to America a year later. After Claus was already dead."

"Oh." Kit took a swallow of tea. "I see."

Sally sat down her cup and cocked her head to one side. "I think I hear Clara." She heaved herself out of the chair. "I better go check."

Kit picked up the cups. She took them to the sink and washed them, then stacked them neatly in the drainer. Her thoughts were with her aunt, lying in her drugged sleep, her fear only temporarily banished from her mind. Why had her nightmares started up after all this time? Kit frowned. Was she to blame? Aunt Augusta didn't start having the bad dreams until just after Kit arrived. Somehow, they were her fault.

She shook her head. Something was wrong. The pieces still did not fit together. What was she missing? Where did Edmund fit into this distorted picture?

She remembered then the picture of Edmund in the photo album. Wiping her hands, she went into the dining room. She had returned the albums to Gramma Clara's room, but now they were once again on the sideboard.

Flipping through them, she found the picture of a young Augusta beside a handsome, blond-haired dandy with a twisted smile. When she had first seen the picture, she had mistakenly thought the young man was Lars—but later, at the dining table, Lars had pointed to this same picture and identified the man as his father. That made more sense, after all, for Lars was much younger than Augusta. Kit bent closer to the photograph, tracing Edmund's long blond mustache with a trembling finger.

The mustache. Could it be that Edmund played a part not only in her aunt's most recent nightmare, but in the previous one as well? Kit remembered her aunt's description of her first bad dream, the cold, slimy, yellow thing that looked like her doll's hair. . . Without knowing it, could her aunt have been describing Edmund's mustache?

Kit shook her head. She was letting her imagination run away with her again, surely. At any rate, she could not mention her suspicions to her aunt, or anyone else in the house for that matter. Still. . .if Aunt Augusta *was* dreaming about Uncle Edmund. . .could he have played some part in Claus' death?

Again Kit shook her head. Edmund would have had to have come to America long before he claimed to have been here. Gramma Clara, Sally, Augusta—they had all agreed that Uncle Edmund had not come until a year after Claus' death. But suppose they hadn't known. . .

Kit's stomach churned. She had read too many mysteries, she told herself. This wasn't like a book she could lay aside anytime she chose, though; this was all too real. Her fear left a tangible taste inside her mouth.

She would have liked to retreat to her bedroom, but she didn't want to disturb her aunt. So. . .she must push forward. The phrase sprang into her memory from the days when Dr. Ellis and her physical therapist had persuaded her to walk again. When she would have been too timid to take the risk, they coaxed her, encouraged her, even raged at her.

"Push forward. Step out. Step forward. Don't be afraid. I won't let you fall, I'll catch you. Step forward in faith. You can do it. Just trust."

Kit smiled. She heard the voice so clearly inside her head. She knew, though, that this time she didn't hear Dr. Ellis' voice, but Another's. "Trust Me," whispered the Voice again.

She remembered how she had felt when she at last tottered forward, first on full-length leg braces and crutches, then crutches alone, then only one crutch, and then at last . . .truly walking, all by herself. She had done it. "Trust me," Dr. Ellis had said, and he had not let her down.

She heard another voice then echoing those same words; "Trust me," said Keith Long, his cool gray eyes smiling. She shook her head and smiled ruefully; just thinking of him made her palms sweaty and her heart race. The force of her longing shook her with its desperation. She longed to hear his voice, to see his face, and most of all, she longed to feel the strength of his arms around her, the warm comfort of him against her face.

She blushed. "What nonsense!" she said out loud. "You have to stop this, girl. Get a grip."

She pulled her thoughts away from Keith—and found herself once more gripped by fear of the strange force that ruled this house. She felt as though she were being sucked down into some mysterious, dark vortex. "If only Keith were here with me," she murmured.

"Trust Me!" The words inside her head were no longer a whisper.

Kit bowed her head. "Lord, You know how alone I feel. I'm afraid. I don't know what I should do. Help me to trust You. Give me courage and wisdom. In Your Son's name, amen."

Stillness settled gently over her heart. Kit lifted her head, and then her chin tipped up even higher. She remembered the stubbornness she had needed to learn to walk again; well, she would be just as resolved now.

As though guided, she walked into the living room and sat down beside Uncle Edmund. "Tell me about your first impressions of America," she said.

Edmund pulled himself straighter in his chair. A small smile played at the corner of his drawn lips as he turned the hourglass between his hands, watching the movement of the sand. "Sweden was home to me no longer," he said at last. "Kat was gone; Clara was in America. So, I came over too."

"And you married?"

"*Ya*. Clara wanted me to settle down. She said I must . . .what could I do? I married to please Clara. It was the least I could do."

Kit made a face, trying to keep her feelings from show-ing too plainly. "You married someone just to please your sister?"

Uncle Edmund sniffed. "Didn't work, though. Clara didn't like Lizzy. I never could please my saintly sister, never. She was always against me."

"That's not what I've heard. I understand that Gramma Clara tried to protect you when you got in trouble."

Her uncle snorted. "Who told you that? I wasn't such a bad lad, not like they make out. High-spirited, *ya*. Clara shouldn't have sided with Kat against me. . .shouldn't have taken what belongs to me." The old man's eyes glit-tered, and Kit heard the rasp of his teeth against each other.

"Gramma would never take what didn't belong to her," Kit protested.

"You think not." Edmund laughed. "Maybe you don't know your grandmother as well as you think you do." He looked at Kit, his face sly. "You're not so innocent your-self, are you? I know what you came for. . .and you won't get it." He stuck his face closer to Kit's. "You hear? You won't get it!"

Kit got to her feet. "I told you before—I came here only because Gramma asked for me. You keep her estate. I for one wish she could live forever, even if you do not." She bit her lip, realizing what her words implied.

Edmund's glittering eyes narrowed to slits. "You think I wish my sister to die, is that it? Well, you're wrong. What chance then would I have of getting back my own?"

Kit looked down at the old man. "What does Gramma have of yours that's so important? Why don't you just ask her for whatever it is?"

Edmund looked away. "This is not your concern. I see you don't believe me. Nevertheless, Clara has something which is rightfully mine."

"Why hasn't she returned it to you then?"

The old man shrank back into his chair, and his voice fell to a mumble. "What do a couple of pieces of paper matter to her?"

Kit shifted her weight. "So why are they so important to you? What are they?" She waited for a long moment, and when Edmund did not respond, she repeated, "What are they?" But Edmund only smiled vaguely. Kit sighed, and decided to try a different approach. "I suppose you helped Claus with the farm when you first arrived."

Edmund shot forward in his chair. Even Lars put down the newspaper he was reading and stared at his father. "I didn't!" Edmund shouted. "He stole my Kat, and then my sister. Help him? Why, I. . ." He slumped back in his chair, and then he whined, "How could I help Claus? He was already long buried by the time I arrived."

Kit shrugged. "I guess I still haven't gotten the family history properly sorted out in my mind. Maybe you could help me get things straight?" She waited, but she heard only the old man's heavy breathing. He was either ignoring her or he had sunk once more into the past. Still, she imagined she could feel hate emanating from him like a dark cloud, and panic rose in her throat.

"Nice try," Lars snorted, "but you won't get anything more out of him now. Doesn't even know you exist." He turned back to his paper, as though he too would wipe out her existence.

Kit left the living room, considering Uncle Edmund's words. *Had* he been in America before Claus died? It was high time, Kit thought, to talk to Gramma Clara again.

Back in the bedroom, she found Augusta trying to adjust the crutches beneath her sore arms. Kit watched her, then suggested, "Try to put more weight on your hands rather than under your arms."

Augusta repositioned her weight and took a tentative step. "*Tack sa mycket.* It does help. Thank you, Kit."

Augusta made her way slowly to the bathroom. Watching her, Kit bit her lip, praying her aunt would not fall. She sighed in relief when Augusta reached the bathroom door, but as Kit turned away a crash made her spin back so fast she nearly fell.

"Sally! Sally!" Kit screamed.

Surprisingly, Lars sauntered in from the living room, but Sally was the one who helped a white and shaken Augusta back to her feet. "Get those crutches, Lars," Sally ordered over her shoulder.

Reluctantly, Lars reached and picked them up from the floor. His thick lips twisted, he watched as Sally led Augusta back into the bedroom. Then he turned on his heel and went briskly back into the living room.

Kit stared after him, her hands clenched in fists at her sides. She turned back toward the bathroom door, and then she frowned. Something. . .something about the way her aunt had fallen. . . Kit had turned in time to catch a glimpse of her aunt catapulting forward. When Kit had fallen when she had first begun using crutches, she hadn't fallen like that. . .not with such forward momentum. She took a step closer to the bathroom door, then stared down in horror.

A nearly invisible cord was strung across the threshold, just high enough for someone to catch their toe under. A deliberately set trap. But for who?

One thing was certain, Aunt Augusta had once again suffered a manufactured "accident." But who was the intended victim? And what would happen next?

Lars. Somehow Kit was certain that Lars played a part in this. She was as sure as. . .well, she was almost sure.

But whoever was to blame, she could no longer blame her own imagination for interpreting innocent events wrongly. She stared down at the cord that spanned the bathroom doorway. This time, the danger in this house was undeniable.

And this time, she *knew* she needed someone's help and advice.

eleven

This is the dream; and we will tell the interpretation thereof before the king. Daniel 2:36

❧

A weak voice disturbed Kit's thoughts. Gramma. She tiptoed into her grandmother's room. "What can I do for you, Gramma?" She thought Gramma Clara looked worse than before. Her fragile skin was nearly transparent now, her gaze unfocused, as though years had elapsed since Kit last saw her.

Her grandmother struggled to speak. "Noise," she said at last. "What happened?"

So this time she had heard the commotion. "Aunt Augusta fell. She'll be fine, though, don't worry. Just shook herself up. Sally is with her." Kit could not bring herself to tell her grandmother what she had discovered.

Gramma frowned. "That's strange. Odd she should fall again." She groped for Kit's hand. *"Var snall och var forsiktig.* Please be careful." Her hand dropped back onto the bed covers and her eyes fell shut.

Kit turned to leave, but before she could get to the door, she heard her grandmother's voice again. "Wait!"

Kit turned back to the bed. "I'm here, Gramma."

"Augusta is all right? You're certain?"

Kit nodded. "She was dazed—but otherwise she seemed fine."

"Did she have. . .another nightmare today?"

"Yes. How did you know?"

Gramma Clara turned her head away, but not before Kit saw the fear in her faded eyes.

"Gramma, what's wrong?"

"Help her, Kit," the old woman whispered. "Don't let her remember. For all our sakes, don't let her remember. It may. . ." Her voice trailed away, and Kit leaned close to catch the last word. She thought she heard, *"Varning."*

Varning. The ominous word followed Kit as she left her grandmother's room. Warning. Needing to be alone to think, Kit went out the back door to the small porch. It was little more than a hot, stuffy closet, with one small window that showed the brown lawn simmering under the burning sun. The flowers that lined the yard, obviously planted with care by Augusta, were shriveling, dying. . .like Gramma Clara. Despite the heat, Kit shivered.

Overhead, a few robins lit on the high telephone wires; then suddenly, as one, they fluttered and flew away. At the same instant, Kit gasped.

All this time, she had seen Aunt Augusta as Gramma Clara's protector. But what if. . .what if Kit had it backwards?

Was Gramma instead the protector? Did Augusta hold a secret inside her mind so devastating that someone would seek to do her harm rather than have the secret revealed? Had Gramma Clara protected her daughter the only way she could, by imposing the years of silence and secrecy?

If that were true, Kit realized, then she was to blame for Augusta's injuries. Kit was the one who had made her aunt remember—and now someone was trying to hurt Augusta. All of Kit's doubts about her own worth came rushing back. "Oh, God, why do I always mess things up?"

"Trust Me."

The voice inside her head startled her. She swallowed her tears. "Help me," she whispered.

"Trust Me," the voice repeated.

Kit bowed her head. "I will. I will." This was no time, she realized, to muck about in self-pity. The dangerous memories were already surfacing, and everyone in the house knew they were. Gramma Clara could no longer protect her daughter with secrecy. Somehow, Kit knew she had to find the answer. Only by exposing the long hidden secret would her aunt be free now—and safe.

Who knew the secret? Gramma Clara did, she was sure. And somewhere in her subconscious, so did Aunt Augusta. Uncle Edmund possibly—but surely he was too old and weak to have set the traps. Lars? He had not even been born when Claus died, but perhaps he had found out something. . . But why would he care?

From inside the house, Kit heard the phone ring. She went back through the kitchen to answer it.

"How you doing?" Keith's deep voice made her face brighten.

"Keith. . .Dr. Long." She took a deep breath. "I'm so glad you called. I was thinking of calling you later."

"Well, you know what they say about great minds thinking alike." She heard the smile in his voice.

"Right." Kit took another breath, forcing herself to relax. "How's the conference?"

"Pretty boring, actually." He hesitated, then said abruptly, "I'd like to see you again."

Kit stopped breathing. "I'd like to see you too," she managed to squeak.

"How about that date to Valley Fair? You will go with me, won't you?"

Kit sank down on the chair beside the phone. He was only teasing, she reminded herself, he didn't mean a real date, the kind between a man and a woman. He was only doing his Christian duty, fulfilling his promise to Dr. Ellis. She squeezed her eyes shut. "When?"

He heard the anxiety and hesitation in her voice. "Are you all right?" he snapped. "Has something happened you're not telling me?"

Desperately, Kit longed to confide her fears and suspicions, but this was neither the time nor place. She could not risk someone overhearing her, and she did not want to hold the doctor up too long. "I'm all right," she said. "Aunt Augusta sprained her ankle. And then a little while ago she fell with her crutches." She clutched the phone, praying Keith would not hang up yet. "When will I see you?"

"How does tomorrow afternoon sound?"

"Fine."

Her voice sounded forlorn. Keith pressed his lips together, frustrated that he could not comfort her. "I have to go, Kit." His voice was gentle. "I'm on a pay phone. . ."

"Yes, of course. Thank you for calling."

"Kit." He could not bear to let her go.

"Yes?"

"I'll be praying for you."

"Thank you. I. . .I need it."

"Tomorrow then."

"Tomorrow," Kit echoed. She hung up the phone, trying to choke back the lump in her throat. As soon as Keith's voice was no longer in her ear, her fear hit her again full force, leaving her trembling.

She went back to the bedroom. Her aunt lay on her bed, still and white, her eyes so glassy that Kit was frightened even more. "Aunt Augusta, what is the matter?"

Sally put a finger to her lips. "I'm afraid, dearie," she whispered, "that this has all been too much for her. I'm afraid she's headed for another breakdown. I gave her something to calm her, but. . ."

Kit followed the nurse out into the kitchen to help her prepare dinner. "Will she be all right?"

"No way of knowing, dearie. Be a shame to have to put her away again. This time, without Clara, I doubt she'd ever get out."

Kit twisted the gold bracelet on her arm. "She has to get better then," she said firmly.

Sally shook her head. "I don't think you understand how far your aunt is from being stable, how far she always has been."

"I think," Kit retorted, "Aunt Augusta would be fine— if someone didn't keep manufacturing 'accidents' for her."

Sally swung her bulk around and looked at Kit. "Just what are you saying?"

"I'm saying that Aunt Augusta didn't just fall this time— anymore than she did the first time."

"What do you mean?"

"Someone strung a cord across the bathroom threshold. That's why she tripped."

Sally's eyes showed her doubt. "Come on now, dearie. Don't let that imagination of yours work overtime."

"I'll show you. I saw the cord." Kit led Sally out into the hall to the bathroom.

"I don't see anything," Sally said.

The cord was gone.

"But it was right here."

Sally patted Kit's shoulder, her chubby face smiling. "There, there, dearie. It's all right."

Kit moved away from the nurse's hand. "I did see it!"

"Of course, dearie. I'm sure you did. Now, why not lie down for awhile before dinner?"

Kit ground her teeth, but she limped into the bedroom without saying anything more. She sank down on the edge of the bed. Augusta was breathing slowly and deeply, her face turned toward the wall. "Please help Aunt Augusta be all right," Kit whispered. "Me too. Keep us safe through this night."

Tomorrow afternoon seemed like an eternity away, but she clung to the promise of once more being with Keith. Would he doubt her story like Sally had? Kit knew the cord had been there, that it had not been her imagination. Someone had removed it. . .

Maybe the object was not so much to harm Augusta but to drive her over the edge. Was someone so greedy for Gramma's estate? And what of herself? Both Uncle Edmund and Lars believed she had come to claim her share in the inheritance. Surely they did not think they could drive her away with childish pranks. But, she reminded herself, that loose step had not been childish. It had injured and frightened Aunt Augusta, but it could have killed Kit.

Hugging her arms to her chest, Kit shivered. "Keith," she whispered, "I need you. I don't know what to do. Oh, what should I do?"

She winced, realizing she sounded like her indecisive aunt, and squared her shoulders. She would manage. After all, God was with her.

But she wished she could convince Sally. Then she wouldn't feel so alone. But Sally was so used to dealing with sick people that she naturally saw illness as an explanation for anything out of the ordinary. That left Keith . . .tomorrow.

God was with her now, though. He knew what was going on, even if she didn't. She reached for her Bible.

She read for a long time, soaking up Proverbs like a sponge. When at last she closed the Bible, the verses from Proverbs 3:5 and 6 lingered in her mind: "Trust in the Lord with all thine heart; and lean not unto thine own understanding. In all thy ways acknowledge him, and he shall direct thy paths."

Trust. It was so hard to trust. . .Kit's thoughts drifted, and her eyes fell shut. Trust. . .

Keith stood beside her, holding her hand. "I love you, Kit. Trust me. Trust God." In her sleep, Kit smiled.

Sally's call to dinner woke her. She shook her head as she remembered the dream, trying to dismiss it from her mind, but joy danced inside her, refusing to be squelched.

Augusta was already awake. She had dressed for dinner and now was patting her hair in front of the mirror. Her eyes had lost their glassiness, but her expression was still bewildered.

"How are you feeling?" Kit ran a brush through her own long hair.

"Much better, thank you." Augusta put her crutches under her arms.

Kit watched her thoughtfully, not sure if she should tell her about the cord. At last she decided that telling her aunt would do more harm than good. If only Augusta could tell her why someone would want to harm her. . .

Her aunt needed to remember. . .but was it worth the risk to her sanity? Surely, though, she was already riding the edge, even without the knowledge. Hadn't God promised that the truth would set people free? But in her aunt's case. . .

Kit took a deep breath. "Aunt Augusta, what do you

remember about the night your father died?"

Her aunt froze. "No. No! I don't remember anything."

"Do you think you might if you really tried?" Kit pulled on her blue dress. She fastened a wide white belt around her waist, slipped flat white shoes on her feet.

"Maybe," her aunt answered at last. "But they told me not to, so I've never tried. They said I mustn't."

"Forget what they said," coaxed Kit. "Do you remember your father's heart attack?"

Augusta trembled, then sat down suddenly on the bed. "It was my fault. He got sweaty, weak. He begged me to get his pills. I was always so proud to help him. . ." She bit her lip.

"So you brought the pills."

Augusta's upper lip shone with sweat. "I. . .I think so. . ."

"You gave them to your father," Kit encouraged. She watched her aunt carefully. Augusta still shook, but she did not appear to be losing control. Maybe she was stronger than anyone gave her credit for being. Maybe the only reason she had never been able to put the incident behind her was because no one would let her talk about it. Hidden away, the memory had festered in her heart. Kit put her hand on her aunt's shoulder; she knew what a hidden wound could do to your image of yourself, for she had only recently exposed her own hurt. She sat down on the bed beside her aunt.

Augusta closed her eyes, and Kit prayed no one would interrupt them. She watched her aunt take a deep breath. "Yes. . .no. I. . .I was too. . .too late." She opened her eyes and stared up at Kit. "You understand? I was too late."

"Were you and Gramma the only ones with your father that night?"

"Yes. . .I think. . ." Suddenly, Augusta's eyes flew wide,

then quickly closed.

Kit leaned forward. "What is it, Aunt Augusta? What do you remember?" She reached her hand out to her aunt, but Augusta pushed it away.

"Nothing. I remember nothing." Terror stared from her tight face.

"All right," Kit soothed, "all right." But her aunt had obviously remembered something. Whatever it was had terrified her.

"Hey, you two," Sally called through the door. "Didn't you hear me call you for dinner?"

"We'll be right there," Kit answered.

Augusta struggled quickly to her feet and clumped out to the dining room, as though afraid that Kit would hold her back with more questions. Kit followed her, smiling as she saw that her aunt had at last mastered the crutches. Kit's smile faded; she would have to watch carefully for anymore traps.

When Kit and Augusta joined them, the others were already seated around the table. Kit slid into her chair, and surreptitiously watched the others as she ate. Uncle Edmund kept his head down. Lars wore his usual smirk. Sally was chatting cheerfully with Aunt Augusta, while her aunt answered in hesitant monosyllables. An eerie calm seemed to have settled over everyone, like the stillness before a tornado.

To Kit's relief, Uncle Edmund and Lars left immediately after dinner. Sally and her aunt lingered at the table, sipping tea and nibbling on eclairs. Kit excused herself and went to her bedroom.

She swung her suitcase onto the bed and snapped it open. The jewelry box was still safe. She sat down on the bed, holding the box in her lap. Her fingers caressed the smooth wood. How could this little box hold the secret that swirled through this house?

Why had Gramma asked her to bring the box with her, when she had never even asked to see it? And why had Gramma made her promise not to talk about the box to anyone? Someone knew, though, that was obvious. What connection could the box possibly have to her aunt's "accidents"?

Sighing, Kit opened the lid. The box had been in the family so long; surely, any secret it might have held would have long since been discovered. Was that it? The secret, whatever it was, no longer existed, and that made someone angry?

Kit frowned. She poked her finger along the box's velvet interior, feeling carefully. For a moment, she almost thought she heard her namesake Katalina calling to her from the past—but that was silly. Still, Kit had a strong sense of being guided.

Down in one corner of the box, she uncovered a tiny screw. None of the other corners had one. Her hand shaking, she reached into her cosmetics bag and found a nail file. Very carefully, she tried to turn the screw.

It would not budge. Kit gritted her teeth, then wrapped both hands around the nail file. Ever so slightly, she felt the screw give, then it popped up like a tiny handle. Kit pulled it gently. The entire velvet-covered bottom came away in her hand.

Beneath it, inside the small secret compartment, Kit saw some pieces of paper. Her hands shaking even more, she pulled out four sheets of thin, folded paper. Carefully, gently, afraid they might disintegrate in her hands, she unfolded them.

Hand-printed sheet music. Four songs by—Kit squinted

to read the faded ink—A.L. Augustafson.

Trying to still her trembling hands, Kit refolded the music and hid it once more in its compartment in the jewelry box. She screwed the secret compartment shut as tightly as she could, her thoughts racing. Then she put the box back in her suitcase and slid the case back behind her bed. How had the music gotten into the box?

A.L. Augustafson had been a legend even while he had been alive, a famous songwriter who became even more well-known after he had become a Christian. Any manuscript of his would have been valuable even during his lifetime, but now. . .the implications staggered Kit.

But who had put the music in the jewelry box? And who knew it was there? Was this why Gramma Clara had asked her to bring the box? And why now? Had someone recently found out about the music, someone who had no right to it?

If only she had a better place to hide the sheets of paper. But whoever had taken the box could not have found the music, or surely they would have taken it.

Kit shook her head. She would have to ask her grandmother to explain. This mystery had gone on far too long. Things were getting out of hand. . .

But she could do nothing more today. Tomorrow. . . tomorrow she would talk with Gramma Clara. And tomorrow she would be with Keith.

twelve

And shall say unto them, Hear, O Israel,
ye approach this day unto battle against your enemies:
let not your hearts faint, fear not, and do not tremble,
neither be ye terrified because of them.

Deuteronomy 20:3

❧

Kit awoke early, nearly as exhausted as when she went to bed. The hot, humid air pressed against her face as she sat up, and she longed for air conditioning. Since she had been here, even the window fan in the living room had not been turned on, as though the inhabitants of this house were somehow immune to the heat.

She got out of bed and pulled open the curtains. Light fell across the other bed, showing Kit her aunt's slack face and one limp arm that hung over the edge of the bed. For once Augusta had not been plagued with nightmares; Sally's pills must have done a good job of putting her to sleep. Kit frowned and looked closer at her aunt's face. Maybe the pills had worked too well. Her aunt seemed almost too relaxed, her sleep too heavy.

Still frowning, Kit picked out a pair of navy pants and a white cotton shirt. She gathered them up and went into the bathroom to shower and dress. Soon Sally would arrive, and once the nurse had Clara dressed and ready for the day, Kit intended to talk to her grandmother.

A half hour later, Kit returned to the bedroom, running a comb through her wet hair. Augusta stood beside her bed, swaying. "I need to check on Mother," she said, her voice thick. She thrust her arms into a robe, then reached for her crutches. "I should have been up an hour ago. I can't imagine why I slept so long. . .oh, dear." She sat down suddenly on the bed and rubbed her forehead. "Has Sally arrived yet? I feel woozy."

Kit looked down at her aunt, and her brow puckered. "Sally should be here any minute. And Gramma must still be asleep. I've been up for a while now, and I haven't heard anything from her room. Don't worry, Aunt Augusta. Go ahead and get dressed. I'll get us some breakfast."

Her aunt shook her head. "Just for yourself, please. I couldn't eat anything. *Tack sa mycket.*"

"You're sure?"

Augusta nodded, and Kit left her to dress in privacy. In the kitchen she made herself a peanut butter and honey sandwich on whole wheat bread, poured herself a glass of milk, and sat down.

The back door opened. "Morning, dearie. How's everything this morning?"

Kit smiled. "Hi, Sally. Aunt Augusta didn't have any nightmares last night."

The nurse set her bulging purse on the table. "Sounds promising. What about your grandmother?"

"She's still sleeping, I guess. I thought I shouldn't wake her."

"That's right. Let her rest. I'd better get in there now, though." She started for the door, then said over her shoulder, "I didn't see Lars' car as I came in. Don't tell me those two wonders haven't shown up yet?"

Kit giggled and shook her head. "Nope."

Sally chuckled and ambled down the hall toward Clara's

room. A moment later, she was back, her smile gone. Her face was white, her eyes wide. Kit set down her sandwich. "What is it?"

"Is Augusta in her room?"

Kit nodded, and the nurse disappeared again. Kit waited, her stomach churning. At last, the two women came in the kitchen, Augusta leaning heavily on Sally. Kit looked at the tears that stained her aunt's face. "Lord, no," she whispered.

She listened while Sally called for an ambulance. "Gramma is worse?" she asked when the nurse had hung up.

Sally took a deep breath and squared her shoulders. "Dearie, your dear grandmother is gone."

"Gone?"

Sally nodded. "She died quietly. In her sleep." She turned to Augusta. "Are you okay?"

Augusta rocked back and forth. "If only I'd checked her," she murmured. "I shouldn't have slept so late. I was too late. . .again."

"Nonsense," Sally answered. "There was absolutely nothing you could have done. Your mother died in her own bed, with no pain, just as she wished."

Kit gripped the edge of the table, feeling weak and sick. She had come to Minneapolis knowing her grandmother had little time left—but still the reality left her shaken, overwhelmed. If only she could have spent more time with Gramma.

From a distance, Kit watched white-coated attendants come and take away her grandmother's small, quiet form. She sat unmoving while Sally helped Augusta out the door to her car. Neither woman spoke to Kit, as though she were invisible, as though she weren't there. Kit shook herself. After all, Sally had enough to see to without having to take care of a cripple.

"Crippled!" she whispered. "Useless!" Tears gathered in her eyes, then rolled down her cheeks. "Why did I come here, God? I haven't been any use. I haven't helped. . . If anything, I've made things worse."

Someone pounded on the front door, and she got slowly to her feet. She let Uncle Edmund and Lars in, brushing at her tears as they pushed past her.

"What's for breakfast?"

Kit stared at them. "Nothing. Gramma Clara is dead."

Edmund put a hand on the wall, his pale face growing still whiter. "She's not still here?"

"No. They took her away a little while ago. Sally and Aunt Augusta went to make the arrangements."

Edmund slumped into his usual chair in the corner. His trembling fingers caressed the hourglass, but he did not pick it up.

Kit put her hands on her hips. "Shouldn't you two get down to the funeral home too? I'm sure Aunt Augusta could use your support right now."

Edmund did not answer, did not appear to have even heard her, but Lars sneered. "Nothing's going to keep old Augusta topside now. By tomorrow they'll have her tucked away in some nice safe rubber room."

Kit's hands clenched into fists, and she bit her teeth together to hold back her anger. She fled to the bedroom and found Keith's card. Her hand shaking, she dialed the number, praying he would still be there.

"Hello?" It was his sister's voice.

"Is Dr. Long there?" She tried to keep her voice from trembling.

"Kit! Is that you? I'm sorry. He left early this morning.

Today's the last day of the conference, you know. Can I leave him a message?"

Kit closed her eyes. "Just tell him I called," she whispered. "Gramma's dead." She hung up the phone, feeling as though she would choke on the sense of menace that hung in the heavy air. She had to escape.

She stuck her head in the living room. "I'm going for a walk. If you leave, don't lock the door."

She knew she was stupid to walk alone in the city, knew she was taking a risk. But she had to get out of the house. She had to think.

Her disappointment at not being able to talk to Keith was too great, she told herself. She longed for the comfort of his presence, his skeptical face, his warm arms . . .but surely that was only to be expected at a moment like this, when Gramma had just died. Of course, she would long for sympathy and understanding. . .and love.

Love? Keith Long did not love her, she knew that, so where had that word come from? They had only known each other a short time, too short a time for love to have grown, even if such a thing were possible. Love did not burst into being out of no where, did it?

And yet, she recognized, it had. She knew she was foolish to even imagine that he could ever love her—but nevertheless, she had grown to love him. The feeling had not grown out of nothing either, she realized; it was no shallow infatuation, but the real thing, growing gradually ever since the first time she met him, fed by their long talks, by his warmth and consideration. "I love him," she said softly, dazed by the realization. "No matter what, I love him."

"As I love you," whispered a small voice inside her mind.

Kit lifted her face to the cloudless sky. "You love me, God. No matter what, You love me."

She took a deep breath. Gramma Clara would never now explain the secret—but Kit knew her job was still to solve the mystery. Otherwise, Aunt Augusta would never be safe.

Questions buzzed in her mind, but she had no answers. Frustrated, she bowed her head and committed the problem to her loving Father. This new love she had for Keith had helped her understand for the first time that God truly did love her.

Peace settled over her. She turned and went back to the house.

Inside, the house had a strangely empty feel. Neither Lars nor Uncle Edmund was in the living room, nor were they in the kitchen or dining room. Kit shrugged and checked the bathroom, then glanced at her grandmother's door. She gulped, then looked inside.

"Oh, no!" Someone had destroyed Clara's room. The sheets on the bed had been slashed, the blankets ripped off and strewn across the floor. Broken china lay everywhere amid scattered papers and books. Kit ran from the room, hugging her arms around her chest.

Had someone been looking for the manuscripts? The house had been left unlocked, but surely this couldn't have been a random looting. Could it?

She picked up the phone to call the police, then hesitated. What if a family member had done this? If only she could talk to Keith. He would know what to do. She could have him paged at the conference, she supposed, but she shrank from the idea.

"Lord," she whispered. "I know You love me. You said to trust You. Well, I need some help now."

The phone under her hand trilled, making her jump. Her heart pounding, she picked it up. "Hello?"

"Kit, are you all right?"

Kit let out her breath in a long sigh. "Oh, Keith. Thank goodness."

"What's wrong?"

"My grandmother died. I had to get out, so I went for a walk. When I returned. . .someone had ransacked her room." She swallowed. "Oh, Keith, ever since I got here, such weird things have been happening. I'm here by myself now, but I'm. . .I'm scared."

"Kit, hang on. I'll be there as soon as I can. Are you sure no one is in the house with you now?"

"Pretty sure. Just a minute, I'll check." She set the phone down, and missed the doctor's order to wait. While she checked the house's lower floor, he prayed for her safety.

He was sweating by the time she picked up the phone again. "Keith—"

"What a foolish thing to do!" he interrupted. "Don' you have more sense than to go looking for trouble? Wha if there had been a burglar in the house?"

"But I thought. . ." Tears sprang to her eyes. "You said . . . I thought you wanted me to. . ." His anger bewildered her.

Keith heard the break in her voice, and he forced him self to be calm. "Kit, I want you to lock yourself in. Prom ise me. I'll get there as soon as I can. And Kit—God wil take care of you."

Reluctantly, he hung up the phone. He could do her no good as long as he was here at the conference center, he knew, but he hated to cut the connection between them hated to be out of touch with her for the time he would need to drive to her aunt's house.

As he strode down the corridor, he was seeing Kit's small face, her blue eyes wide with fright, and he nearly collided with one of his colleagues.

"Excuse me," he said absently.

"That's all right. You're Dr. Long, aren't you?" The woman's smile invited him to linger.

Keith glanced at the woman's lush figure; he knew her to be articulate and intelligent, the embodiment of his ideal woman. He felt nothing toward this woman, he realized, nothing at all. In that instant, he mentally tossed in the garbage his list of requirements for a perfect woman.

He did not want the perfect woman after all. No. He shook his head, hardly able to believe his own thoughts. He wanted, he needed, a small, imperfect, sometimes confused woman, one who had a living faith. He wanted Kit.

His face set, he turned in the direction of the parking garage. A hand on his shoulder stopped him.

"Dr. Long, good! I'm glad you're still here. We have an emergency situation on our hands. We need your expertise. Now."

❧

As Kit replaced the phone in its cradle, Sally and Augusta came through the door. Sally took one look at Kit's face. "What's wrong? What else has happened?"

"Come and see." Kit led the way to Clara's room. At least now, Sally could not accuse her of imagining things.

Augusta's hand flew to her mouth. "Oh, oh, oh."

"What happened here, dearie?" Kit heard a note of accusation in the nurse's voice.

"Isn't it obvious? Someone searched Gramma's room. I left Lars and Uncle Edmund here. When I returned, they were gone—and the room was like this."

Anger flashed in Sally's usually placid face. "You left?

Where did you go?"

"Out for a walk."

Augusta's eyes widened. "You mean they left the door unlocked? Why, anything might have happened. They should have known better."

Kit flushed. "I'm afraid that's my fault. I asked them not to lock the door if they left. After all, I have no key."

"Whyever would you go out for a walk alone? You know what I told you."

"I know, Aunt Augusta. I'm sorry. I just had to get out for a little while."

Sally frowned at Kit. "Thanks to your thoughtlessness, dearie, a prowler was able to enter the house."

Kit shook her head. "That doesn't make any sense. If it was a burglar who did this, why didn't he take anything valuable? The silver tea set is still in the dining room, the Sevres china. . . It doesn't make any sense at all."

Augusta took a deep breath, obviously struggling to regain her composure. "The police. Should we call the police?"

Sally shook her head. "What good would it do? As Kit says, apparently nothing was taken. Whoever it was won't be back. And no one," she looked at Kit with narrowed eyes, "will be so foolish as to leave the door unlocked again. No, Augusta, right now, with your mother awaiting burial, police interference would only make more trouble." She put her hand on Augusta's shoulder. "Might be a long time before you could get back to normal," she added heavily.

"Are you sure. . .? Of course, you're right. I couldn't bear any more. . .not right now."

Sally's grip on Augusta's shoulder tightened. "Come, Augusta, let me help you lie down. Everything is going to be fine. This is a hard time, naturally, but things will be all right. Trust me."

Augusta pulled back. "No. I can't lie down now. I have calls to make."

Sally hesitated. "Well. . .go ahead then, if you have to. But afterward, you must lie down." She looked around the ravaged room and heaved a sigh. "I best clean this mess up." She picked up a blanket and began to fold it. "By the way, Augusta, you don't have any of Clara's things in your room do you? I might as well get all her things tidied away, while I'm at it."

Augusta shook her head. "You know how Mother wanted her things around her. I don't think I have anything in my room." She sat down by the phone and picked up the receiver.

Kit watched while Sally's wide shoulders stretched to strip the ruined sheets off the bed. "I'll help you, Sally," she offered.

"No, dear," the nurse answered, not bothering to turn around. "I'd rather do it myself."

Once, Kit would have read her own lack of worth into a refusal like that, but now she knew how much God valued her. After all, hadn't He sent His Son to die for her?

"I'll fix us some lunch then," she said and went down the hall to the kitchen.

A few minutes later the three women sat silently around the table, each one so deep in their own thoughts that they might as well have been three strangers. Kit sensed the other women's condemnation, and she sighed. They were right; she had been foolhardy to go out alone, leaving the house unlocked.

Sally pushed back her plate and picked up her coffee cup. "I suppose you'll be making plans now to return home," she said to Kit. "Did you ever find out why Clara wanted to see you so badly?"

Kit swallowed the last bite of her salad. She shook her head. "No, I never did. Mostly, whenever I had the chance to talk to her, she just reminisced about the past." Kit hesitated. "She did say one strange thing the last time I talked to her. Something like *varning*."

Augusta's head jerked up. "Are you certain you heard correctly, Kit?"

"I think so. It means warning, doesn't it?"

Her aunt nodded. "Whyever should Mother say such a thing to you?"

Sally shrugged. "I wouldn't put much stock in it. Clara was dying. Like as not, her mind wandered a bit."

Kit doubted that, but she did not contradict the nurse. Augusta too looked doubtful. She shook her head, then sat up straight. "Wait a minute. Kit, Mother left something for you. She gave it to me yesterday."

"She did?" Sally and Kit spoke at the same time.

Augusta nodded. "Let me get it."

Sally heaved herself to her feet. "Let me get it, Augusta. Where is it?"

"It's a letter," Augusta explained. "I put it in my drawer."

Sally returned a moment later with the folded note in her hands. She handed it to Kit. "Go ahead. Read it."

Kit opened it, then passed it to her aunt. "Please. It's in Swedish."

"Mother never did learn to write English well." Augusta's hand shook as she took the letter. She swallowed, then began to read, "*Var snall och. . .*"

"In English please, Aunt Augusta," Kit begged.

"*Ya*, of course." Augusta frowned while her eyes skimmed the note. "It says, 'Please return music manuscripts to Sweden. They belong in a museum. Be careful. Warning. Love. . .'" Augusta glanced up. "I don't understand. Obviously, you were right, Sally. Mother's mind must have been wandering these last few days."

Kit held out her hand. "May I have the note back? It's Gramma's last—and first—letter to me." She had no intention of revealing her understanding of the message.

Sally looked at Kit with sharp eyes. "Do you know what your grandmother meant, by any chance? Maybe she was more alert than we know."

"I think she knew what she was about," Kit agreed. She tucked the note in the pocket of her pants. "I have an idea . . ." She stopped. She had promised Gramma Clara she wouldn't discuss the jewelry box with anyone. Did her promise still hold now that Gramma was dead?

Besides, her troubles were over now surely. With Gramma gone, she could go home now when Keith did. Maybe Keith would be able to help her decide who to contact about the manuscripts. She sighed and decided to say nothing more to either Sally or her aunt.

She cleaned up the dishes while Sally helped Augusta to her bedroom. As Kit hung up the dishtowel, she heard Lars and Uncle Edmund pounding on the door. Reluctantly, she let them in, wishing they were Keith instead.

Uncle Edmund slunk back to his chair in the living room, but Lars ambled about the house as though he owned it now, poking into drawers, lifting vases, obviously assessing the value of Gramma's inheritance.

His presence drove Kit to the bedroom. She found her aunt asleep, knocked out by Sally's pills. Kit went to her own bed and picked up her Bible, then set it down again restlessly. Through the open door, she heard the hum of low voices, and she wondered who was talking. Surely not Lars and Uncle Edmund; she had never seen them do anything but sit silently together.

She was too tired to go and investigate, though, too hot and listless. She put her head down on the pillow, longing to sleep away the time until Keith arrived.

Instead, the very thought of Keith made her heart pound. She pushed herself up, wide awake once more.

At the same moment, Augusta's eyes flew open and she stared wildly at Kit. "Dear God. Kit, I understand my nightmares. I know who caused Father's death. *Det ar inte mitt fel.* It is not my fault!"

thirteen

Whose hatred is covered by deceit,
his wickedness shall be shewed
before the whole congregation. Proverbs 26:26

Kit got up and closed the bedroom door. "Tell me. Please."

Augusta rubbed her damp forehead. "For so long I've been trying to hide from the past. I was terrified of remembering. I was afraid I would discover I was even more guilty than I thought." Slowly, deliberately, she unlocked her clasped fingers. "You made me take another look at myself, Kit. But I was so frightened when the nightmares started up again." She smiled faintly. "I'm still frightened. But," her voice grew stronger, "I've remembered something very important. That night. . .Mother and Father and I were together, having a pleasant evening, when there was a knock at the door." Augusta's thin face twisted. "It was Uncle Edmund. Mother laughed and pulled him inside. She was happy to see him."

"So your uncle did come to America before your father's death."

"*Ya*. Maybe that is one of the things that had me so confused. Everyone told me he came later. I couldn't understand why he would sometimes appear in my nightmares. But now I know. He *was* there. And he was very angry."

Augusta's brow wrinkled as she struggled to remember. "He insisted Father turn something over to him

153

. . .some papers of some kind, I think."

Kit leaned forward. "Did he say what the papers were?"

"I don't recall. But. . .he started screaming at Father, saying such awful things. Father yelled back. Then. . .then Father clutched his chest. He gasped, sent me for his pills. By the time I returned, though, only moments later, he was dead." Augusta covered her face with her fingers. "Father. . ." She put her head in her hands and sobbed.

Kit let her cry, knowing that these tears had been held back for forty years. "What happened then?" she asked when her aunt was calmer.

"I. . .I'm not sure. I think I fainted. Father and I were very close. . .there he was on the floor. . .it was too much for me. I had my breakdown." Augusta swallowed hard, and then her voice steadied. "By the time Uncle Edmund came to America legally, a year had passed. I was just beginning to recover."

"But you never really forgot, did you? The whole thing was inside you all this time, just waiting to explode. If only you had let it out years ago."

Augusta smiled shakily. "I should have done something, said something. But I was so frightened of going crazy again. If I even mentioned having a dream, Uncle Edmund would look at me like. . ." She shrugged.

"I'll bet he did," Kit said dryly. "As long as you didn't remember, he felt safe." She hesitated. "Aunt Augusta, think about this—your accidents started after your nightmares returned."

Her aunt turned her head and stared at Kit. "What?"

"They weren't accidents, Aunt Augusta. Someone tampered with the step; someone put a cord across the bathroom threshold. I don't know who—but I suspect Lars. Maybe he's trying to protect his father—though there doesn't seem to be any love lost between the two of them."

Augusta's eyes were wide. "Kit." Her breath came fast and hard. "What will we do, Kit?"

"Don't tell anyone what you've remembered. . .not yet."

Her aunt shook her head. "I've kept this inside too long. I'm tired of the secrecy. It's time I settled things with Uncle Edmund."

Kit looked doubtfully at her aunt's determined face. Augusta's indecisiveness was gone—but for both their sakes, she needed to persuade her aunt to wait, to move slowly. "Aunt Augusta—"

But her aunt interrupted her before she could finish. "That man practically destroyed my life with his continual hints about my sanity. I haven't known peace for over forty years. He was the one who persuaded Mother to send me away, I know it. She always protected him." Augusta's voice was hard. "I have to confront him. I have to—" Her voice faltered, and her hand jerked to her head; her face twisted.

"What is it? Are you all right?"

"Headache." Augusta's voice was suddenly slurred.

Before Kit could respond, Sally stuck her head in the bedroom door. "Hungry? I have dinner ready. I know it's early, but neither one of you ate much lunch. I thought you might be ready for a bite."

Augusta glanced from Kit's pants to her own rumpled dress. "I guess it's too late to change for dinner." She stood up and smoothed her dress, then slipped her crutches under her arms. Kit watched her, noticing that she seemed to feel better now.

At the dining room table, Augusta seated herself across from her uncle and lifted her chin high. Kit winced. "Lord," she prayed, "this is in Your hands. I can't keep Aunt

Augusta from talking to Uncle Edmund about the past. So I'm depending on You to keep her safe. Please work things out."

Augusta deliberately stared at her uncle, but he ignored her, his eyes on his plate as he shoveled food in his mouth. Lars, however, watched Augusta with raised eyebrows, smirking. Augusta caught his glance, and she seemed to shrink back into her chair. Her chin trembled.

She turned to Sally, as though seeking reassurance. Smiling, the nurse passed Augusta a bowl of meatballs swimming in mushroom sauce. "Did you sleep well, Augusta? I thought you might sleep longer. . ."

"I slept well, thank you, Sally."

"And what about you, Kit? Did you get some sleep too?"

Kit shook her head. "I couldn't sleep." She glanced at her aunt.

Edmund glanced up at her too then, and Kit saw the rage that burned in his pinched face. She looked from the old man to Lars. Lars returned her look with a cold grin.

Unexpectedly, Lars' derisive gaze brought back all Kit's old self-doubt. She felt small, handicapped, helpless. She closed her eyes. "Jesus, help me."

Instantly, she remembered the unconditional love she felt for Keith, and she was reminded once again of God's unconditional love for her. "Thank You, Lord." Maybe she wasn't strong—but God was.

The silence around the table tonight was tense, uneasy. Kit was relieved when Sally finally shooed them away so she could clean the table. Kit hoped her aunt would retire now to her room.

Instead, Augusta clumped into the living room behind her uncle and Lars. From the doorway, Kit watched her aunt take a seat beside Edmund. Augusta's shoulders slumped, and then she took a deep breath and deliberately straightened them. Her fingers twined and untwined, and then she took another deep breath.

"Uncle Edmund, were you in America before Father died?"

Edmund's eyes shot to Augusta's face. "You're sounding strange again, Augusta," he growled.

"No. I'm not. I know you were here before he died."

"How could you know that? Unless. . ." His voice faltered. "Stop!"

Lars leaned forward on the sofa, his eyes swiveling between his father's face and Augusta's.

"You were there. I know you were there." Augusta's voice grew louder, stronger. Edmund seemed to shrink beneath her accusations.

"*Ya*," he said at last. "I was there. I was there."

"You killed my father!" Augusta's voice was shrill now.

"No. I only wanted what was mine."

Lars put out a hand, as though to silence his father. Kit watched, gripping the door frame so tightly her fingers ached. She was afraid of the anger she sensed in the room, terrified of what would happen next. . . She heard Sally moving about the kitchen, humming as she worked, and Kit let out her breath in a long sigh, comforted. Surely neither Lars nor Edmund would do anything while Sally was in the house.

Augusta still had not finished. "You wanted papers from Father, didn't you, Uncle Edmund? You accused him of stealing something from you. But my father never stole anything in his life. He was the kindest, gentlest, most honest man I have ever known."

Edmund shook his head, and his eyes had lost their focus. "I only came for what was mine, Clara. Tell the old man. I must have the papers; I will have them. You understand. You know they are mine."

Augusta sucked in a breath. "Stop that, Uncle Edmund. Mother never took anything from you either."

"*Ya*, Clara, why did you take them from me? Why did you leave me?" Edmund's pale eyes narrowed. "You're no angel either, you know, Clara."

"At least she never let a man burn to death," Kit blurted. She bit her lip, horrified at herself.

Edmund's head jerked toward her, and his eyes snapped with hatred. "Kat," he spat. "All your fault, Kat. Why do you come back to haunt me? The papers belonged to the old man. I worked for him, slaved. I deserved payment so I took the papers. They belonged to me." He struggled to his feet. "They belonged to me, do you understand? I will have them!"

"Murderer!" screamed Augusta. Edmund stared at her blankly for a moment, then slumped back in his chair.

Sally rushed in from the kitchen. She pushed past Kit and stared around the living room, then gathered Augusta in her arms. She patted Augusta's heaving back. "Hush now," she soothed. The cold glance she shot at Kit over Augusta's shoulder made Kit shiver. "You've done it now," Sally muttered to her as she led Augusta out of the room.

Kit followed Sally to the bedroom, coming through the door in time to see the nurse preparing an injection for Augusta. Sally jumped, and her hands froze.

"Why does she need that?" Kit asked.

Sally turned back to her task. Calmly, she inserted the needle in Augusta's arm, then stepped back and watched as Augusta quickly relaxed against her pillow. A small smile curled the corners of the nurse's mouth. "There, there," she soothed. "You'll be fine, Augusta. Soon you'll be just fine."

Augusta's eyes fell shut, and Sally put the syringe in her bag. "She obviously needed a tranquilizer, dearie." She glanced at Kit. "Maybe you could use one too."

Kit shook her head. "No, thank you. I don't need anything like that. But I think I will lie down for a while."

Sally smiled and patted Kit's cheek. "I'll look in on you later, dearie."

Kit stared at the ceiling above her bed. She was certain the papers Edmund wanted were the ones in the jewelry box. Gramma Clara must have hidden them there long ago, before she gave the box to Kit's mother. All these years, the papers were not even in Clara's possession. But who could have known this besides Gramma Clara herself?

Kit was thankful she had told no one about the papers. When she was once more safely in her own home, she would trust Keith with the secret. Together, they would return the valuable manuscripts to Sweden. In the meantime, she would persuade her aunt to stay with her for a time in Kearney. Once everyone knew the manuscripts were in Sweden, her aunt could safely return home. That would end it. . .wouldn't it?

After an hour, Kit gave up trying to rest. She left her aunt still sleeping and went to the living room. There she found Sally sitting near Edmund, talking to him in a low, fast voice. The nurse glanced up when Kit entered the room.

"Couldn't sleep, dearie?"

Kit shook her head.

"You look pleased about something."

"I'm happy to be going home soon," Kit admitted.

Lars snorted. "Think you're going to get away with

Clara's inheritance, do you?"

"No, I don't," retorted Kit. "I don't care if I don't get a thing."

"Sure." Lars snickered.

"Oh, hush, Lars," Sally commanded.

"I only wanted what was mine," Edmund whined.

Lars swung his head toward Kit, and his lips curled.

Sally also looked at Kit. "Dearie, Edmund wants his papers." The nurse smiled calmly.

Kit froze. "What do you mean?"

Lars' eyes were cold. "We know you have them. We just don't know where you've stashed them."

Kit felt as though the evil in the house was taking shape, closing around her, pressing closer. Lars, it had been Lars all along. Kit turned to Sally, but the nurse's broad face had changed. "Sally?" Kit asked doubtfully.

"I know you have those papers, dearie."

"What makes you think that?" Kit was stalling for time, trying to understand.

"Don't forget—I heard your aunt read Clara's note to you." Sally smiled. "Are you going to fetch them for us— or do you want your things ripped up like Clara's were?"

"Lars did that, didn't he?" Kit realized she was holding her breath and forced herself to release it. "And then you checked the room again when you cleaned up the mess, didn't you, Sally?"

Sally's double chin shook with laughter. "Stop stalling, dearie. Go get the manuscripts. I've been waiting for them far too long. I'm not going to scrape and slave one more minute for your precious aunt."

Kit looked from the nurse's hard face to Uncle Edmund and then to Lars. She turned and limped toward the bedroom. As she passed the phone in the hallway, she reached out her hand. "I wouldn't if I were you," warned Lars' voice from the living room door. Kit went into the bedroom.

Augusta lay unmoving on the bed. Her chest barely moved as she breathed, and her face was drawn and bloodless. Kit stared at her. "Oh, God, what if Sally hadn't simply given her a tranquilizer?"

She lay her hand on her aunt's neck and felt the faint flickering pulse beneath her fingers. "Help me, Lord," she whispered. "Protect Augusta."

If only she weren't handicapped; if only she could run for help. She squared her shoulders. Even if she were handicapped, her mind worked fine, and she would find an answer. She must stay calm.

She glanced at the clock, surprised to see that it was nearly six o'clock. Surely Keith should have been here by now. Where could he be?

Kit took a deep breath and opened her suitcase. She took out the jewelry box and took it back to the living room. Edmund leaned forward when he saw it.

"Why, Kat, you still have the box." He reached out his hands and took it from her, then cradled it against his chest, mumbling. "Kat's jewelry box," he said more clearly, looking up at Sally. "That's where the manuscripts have been all this time. Claus gave it to Clara on their wedding day, she told me, and then she gave it to Sophia."

Lars' gaze flicked to Kit. "Is that why the old lady wanted her to come to Minneapolis?"

"Must have been," Sally answered, her eyes on the box.

"Why didn't you take the manuscripts when you took the box out of my suitcase?" Kit asked. "Couldn't you find them?"

They stared at her. Sally glanced at Lars. He shrugged.

"We didn't know you had the box with you," the nurse said. "We thought Clara must have given you the manuscripts after you got here."

"But someone took my box, then put it back."

"Wasn't us," Lars said. He heaved himself to his feet, then ripped the box from his father's grasp. "I want those papers." He opened the box and stared at the empty velvet lining. "Where are they?" he asked Kit and dumped the box in her hands.

Kit fingered the nail file she had brought with her, but she looked not at the box but at Sally. "How did you get involved, Sally? You're Augusta's friend."

The nurse sniffed. "Oh, I'm a good enough friend to do the family's dirty work. But not good enough to marry into the family. Isn't that right, Edmund? You never married me because Clara didn't approve. She didn't want her brother marrying a mere servant, did she?"

Edmund fidgeted in his chair. "It wasn't that," he whined. "I would have needed a divorce. Clara never liked divorce."

Kit shook her head. Sally had poisoned her own life by focusing on what she didn't have, instead of what she did. Kit swallowed hard, realizing how easily the story could have been her own years down the road. "Thank You," she prayed silently. "Thank You for sending Keith to show me Your love."

Kit fiddled with the screw inside the jewelry box, taking as much time as she could. "How did you find out about the papers?" she asked Sally.

"Edmund told me. He'd given up looking for them years ago. But then when Lars came back, he overheard us talking about them. Lars threatened Clara—but Clara just wearied of him and said nothing. When you showed up, though, I knew something was going on. I knew Clara was up to something."

"I don't understand."

Sally waved her hand impatiently. "Who else could Clara trust? Not that idiot daughter of hers for sure. Like I said, I knew she was up to something. I just couldn't figure out what." Her eyes were narrow slits in her round face. "Then you started digging up the past. And when Augusta started her nightmares again, I knew I'd have to take action."

"So you were behind the 'accidents.' What are you going to do now? Kill her?"

Sally sucked in her breath. The expression on her face froze Kit's blood. "What was in that shot you gave her?" she demanded.

The nurse smiled. "Never you mind, dearie. Let's just say that if dear Augusta does wake up, she won't be quite the same as she was before."

"Bats," chortled Lars.

Kit took a deep breath, feeling suddenly calm and clear-headed. She sensed a strength filling her that was outside her human frailty. As she pulled the tiny screw, she prayed that her timing would be just right.

"How did Gramma Clara ever get a hold of such valuable papers in the first place?" she asked.

Sally licked her wide lips, her face relaxed and pleasant. "Seems Edmund was quite the scoundrel back in Sweden. Why do you think Katalina never trusted him? He kept getting in deeper and deeper trouble. While he was in the army, stationed in Stockholm where the manuscripts were kept in a museum, he stole the papers. He thought he had a perfect right to them, since the old man was dead. But before he could sell them—" Sally paused and her face hardened. "Will you hurry up and get those papers out!"

Kit carefully lifted the false bottom out of the box. "They're old," she said. "I have to be careful. You wouldn't want me to crumble them, would you?" She put her fingers in the bottom of the box. "So what happened?"

"Clara discovered them. She knew who'd taken them of course. She planned on returning them, but Edmund threatened to implicate her—and she always protected her brother, always tried to keep him out of trouble. So she hid them from him until she could figure out what to do. I think she thought she could persuade him to be sensible and return them.

"Then Claus came to Sweden and Clara married him. They returned to America, taking the papers with them. Edmund followed his sister to America, trying to get the manuscripts back from her. Claus' death scared him, though. He was terrified of what Augusta might remember."

Sally held out her hand. "Give them to me now, dearie. They belong to us now. We'll sell them and live the way we deserve to live. So hand them over. *Now*."

Kit held the papers out, but she didn't loosen her grip on them. Sally snatched at them, but Kit held on tight. "Careful," she warned. "If you tear them, they'll be worthless."

Sally hesitated, and Kit edged toward the door.

"Give them to me!" The nurse's face was purple.

Lars lurched to his feet, his shoulders hunched. Kit looked at him coolly. "Come near me and I'll rip them to shreds." She moved still closer to the front door.

Sally's mouth was hard. "Where do you think you'll go? Do you know what will happen to you if you step into the streets at this time of night?"

"I'm not giving you the papers," Kit said firmly. "Not until you call an ambulance for Aunt Augusta."

Reluctantly, Sally made the call. She replaced the receiver and took a step closer to Kit. "Now give them to me, you little idiot."

Kit took another step toward the door. She put her hand on the knob.

"Don't let her escape!" she heard Sally scream at the same time the clock chimed the half hour. Lars lunged toward her and Kit fell.

Far away, she thought she heard the door open. Then . . .only darkness.

fourteen

And call upon me in the day of trouble:
I will deliver thee, and thou shalt glorify me.
Psalm 50:15

Kit opened her eyes. She was lying on the living room sofa, she realized. Keith was bending over her. "How are you feeling?"

She touched her forehead. "My head hurts."

Keith smiled, but she noticed that he stroked her hair with a hand that trembled. "You bashed your head pretty hard on the floor."

She tried to sit up, groaned, and laid back down. "What happened? Where is Aunt Augusta? Is she all right?"

"Shh," Keith soothed. "The ambulance arrived in time. They have your aunt under observation at the hospital. In fact," again Keith smiled faintly, "the ambulance arrived right after I decked that bruiser who had just jumped you."

"Did you really?" Kit laughed, somehow amused by the idea. Her smile faded, however. "You got here in time. I knew you would. I don't know how I knew. . .but I knew."

"I'm sorry I wasn't here sooner." Keith's face was grim. "I got held up at the conference—an emergency situation—but I never dreamed how bad things were here. When I think how close I came to being too late—"

"But you weren't," Kit said firmly. "God was in control."

166

Keith nodded. After a moment, he said, "When the police took those three away, the nurse was cheerfully cursing one and all." Keith shook his head. "And your cousin was offering to tell everything he knew—for consideration of course."

"Of course." Kit wrapped her fingers around Keith's large hand. "You were right, you know. I just needed to trust God. My handicap didn't matter at all when I left things in His hands." Her eyes shone.

"Oh, Kit." Keith looked down at her face and took a deep breath. "I'm sorry I didn't get here before I did. I'm sorry you had to face all that. I had no idea you were in such danger! I was counseling a woman on the verge of suicide—and then when I finally got away, the car I rented broke down." His fingers tightened on hers, and his voice grew husky. "I'm so thankful I got here when I did."

"God took care of me," Kit said softly. "I know now . . .He loves me, no matter what." She blushed suddenly, remembering that her own love for Keith was what had convinced her of God's love for herself. She realized how close Keith was, the fabric of his shirt brushing her bare arms, and she asked quickly, trying to distract herself, "What about Uncle Edmund?"

Keith shook his head. "Poor fellow, he was mumbling and babbling to himself. The police took him away too, but I doubt there'll be charges made against him. From what I saw, I'd say they'll have to institutionalize him."

Kit shut her eyes. "That's what he tried to do to my aunt."

Keith slid his arm around her shoulders. "Feel up to telling me the whole story? All I've gotten so far is bits and pieces."

Kit nodded and slowly began to explain. After a

moment, she fell silent, then said thoughtfully, "Gramma must have had Aunt Augusta take the box out of my suitcase. She probably wanted to make sure the papers were still there. I think she wanted me to return them after she was gone, when Edmund could do nothing to hurt her." Kit struggled to sit up. "The manuscripts! Where are they?"

"On the table. I picked them up off the floor." Keith pulled her a little closer. "So tell me what happened."

Kit gulped, trying to concentrate on the story despite the warmth of him against her. "It all started in Sweden over forty years ago. . ."

As she told him everything that had happened in the last few days, Keith frowned. He finally burst out, "Why didn't you tell me any of this? I would never have left you here. That day I saw you, I knew things weren't right, but I never dreamed. . . Beth would have been happy to have you stay at her house."

Kit shook her head. "I couldn't have left Aunt Augusta. After all, she was the one in danger. Besides, I would have hated to have been in your sister's way."

Keith raised his brows and grinned. "Oh, yeah? Well, guess where you're going now? I've already called Beth. She was horrified when I told her the danger you've been in." Once again, his voice grew husky. "I want to take care of you now, Kit."

"But I'll be perfectly safe here now," Kit argued. She tried to hide the shudder that passed over her when she thought of staying in this house alone.

"Sorry, Kit. I say you're going with me." His grin widened. "Even if I have to carry you."

Kit's eyes glinted. "Why should I obey you, Dr. Long?"

"Because," Keith answered, "I expect nothing less than obedience from my future wife."

"What?" To Keith's consternation, Kit's eyes filled with tears. "Please. . .don't tease me like that."

Keith wrapped his other arm around her and pulled her against his chest. "Why do you think I'm teasing?" he asked softly.

Kit pushed him away. "Because I'm. . .because what I am. . . You don't want someone like me for a wife." She wiped the tears off her cheeks with her fingers.

"I thought you were over this nonsense about not being good enough," he said against her hair. "I love you, Kit. You are a lovely, intelligent woman. I don't care a fig about your handicaps. I love you."

Kit stared at him, her blue eyes wide. His lips touched hers, and then he drew back. When he spoke, his voice was hesitant. "Can you love me back, Kit?"

Tears sparkled in Kit's eyes. "I do. . .I already do!"

Keith let out his breath in a long sigh, and once again his mouth found hers.

At last he chuckled and pulled away. "I had my wife all planned, you know. I knew just how she would look, how she would act, how she would talk. . .then you came along and spoiled it all." He looked down at her and touched the tip of her nose with one long finger. "I don't believe in love at first sight—but ever since I first saw you in Ken's office, you have filled my thoughts. . .and then, as I got to know you better, you filled my heart. Until today, I didn't want to admit even to myself that I loved you."

"I didn't want to admit it about myself either," Kit murmured softly against his shirt. "But I do love you. It seems like a dream. . ."

"It's not, you know. It's God."

Kit pushed herself up. "What about Gramma. . .the funeral. . .the manuscripts. . .?"

"We'll take care of everything together. And when the funeral is over, we're going back to Kearney. . .together."

"Well, of course," Kit said, "that's the way we came." She looked puzzled.

"I mean *together*. Permanently." He pulled her back into his arms, and then he kissed her until her head spun. "Darling, would you mind a small wedding at Beth's church with just her family and us? Very soon. I don't want to let you go again."

Kit took a long, deep breath. "If this is a dream, I hope I never, ever wake up. You're sure. . .?"

"Positive. I love you, darling, and I want you to be mine."

He kissed her again, and Kit knew at last that her handicap really did not matter. "Thank You, God. Thank You for helping me to be strong enough to trust You."

Together she and Keith would see that the manuscripts were returned to Sweden. Kit sighed and snuggled closer in Keith's arms. What a wonderful word: *together*. . .

A Letter To Our Readers

Dear Reader:

In order that we might better contribute to your reading enjoyment, we would appreciate your taking a few minutes to respond to the following questions. When completed, please return to the following:

Rebecca Germany, Editor
Heartsong Presents
P.O. Box 719
Uhrichsville, Ohio 44683

1. Did you enjoy reading *To Be Strong*?
    ☐ Very much. I would like to see more books
       by this author!
    ☐ Moderately
       I would have enjoyed it more if _____

    _____

2. Are you a member of *Heartsong Presents*? Yes   No
   If no, where did you purchase this book? _____

   _____

3. What influenced your decision to purchase this
   book? (Check those that apply.)

    ☐ Cover   ☐ Back cover copy

    ☐ Title   ☐ Friends

    ☐ Publicity   ☐ Other _____

4. On a scale from 1 (poor) to 10 (superior), please rate the following elements.

    ___Heroine   ___Plot

    ___Hero   ___Inspirational theme

    ___Setting   ___Secondary characters

5. What settings would you like to see covered in *Heartsong Presents* books?

_____

_____

6. What are some inspirational themes you would like to see treated in future books?_____

_____

_____

7. Would you be interested in reading other *Heartsong Presents* titles?   ❏ Yes   ❏ No

8. Please check your age range:
❏ Under 18   ❏ 18-24   ❏ 25-34
❏ 35-45   ❏ 46-55   ❏ Over 55

9. How many hours per week do you read? ————

Name _____

Occupation _____

Address _____

City _____ State _____ Zip _____

Classic Fiction for a New Generation

Pollyanna
and
Pollyanna Grows Up

Eleanor H. Porter's classic stories of an extraordinary girl who saw the good in everyone. . . and made everyone feel good about themselves.

___Pollyanna___— An orphan dutifully taken in by her repressive aunt, the well-heeled Miss Polly Harrington, Pollyanna Whittier reinvents a game of her father's and finds a way to hide her tears. No one can resist Pollyanna for long and soon almost everyone is playing "the Glad Game," everyone except Aunt Polly. BTP-65 $2.97

___Pollyanna Grows Up___—Ruth Carew's refined Boston world has just been turned upside down. The reason, of course, is obvious: Pollyanna Whittier has come to visit. From Boston to Beldingsville to Europe and back again, *Pollyanna Grows Up* continues the adventures of an irrepressible American girl on the brink of womanhood at the turn of the century. In everything she does—especially the Glad Game—Pollyanna reflects the boundless love of her Heavenly Father. BTP-80 $2.97

.... Presents ....

Great Inspirational Romance at a Great Price!

Heartsong Presents books are inspirational romances in contemporary and historical settings, designed to give you an enjoyable, spirit-lifting reading experience. You can choose from 96 wonderfully written titles from some of today's best authors like Colleen L. Reece, Brenda Bancroft, Janelle Jamison, and many others.

When ordering quantities less than twelve, above titles are $2.95 each.

SEND TO: Heartsong Presents Reader's Service
               P.O. Box 719, Uhrichsville, Ohio 44683

Please send me the items checked above. I am enclosing $ _____
(please add $1.00 to cover postage per order. OH add 6.5% tax. PA and
NJ add 6%.). Send check or money order, no cash or C.O.D.s, please.
       To place a credit card order, call 1-800-847-8270.

NAME _____

ADDRESS _____

CITY/STATE _____ ZIP _____